Never Laugh as a Hearse Goes By

ALSO BY ELIZABETH J. DUNCAN

A Small Hill to Die On
A Killer's Christmas in Wales
A Brush with Death
The Cold Light of Mourning

Never Laugh as a Hearse Goes By

A PENNY BRANNIGAN MYSTERY

Elizabeth J. Duncan

Minotaur Books

A Thomas Dunne Book

New York

A THOMAS DUNNE BOOK FOR MINOTAUR BOOKS.
An imprint of St. Martin's Publishing Group.

NEVER LAUGH AS A HEARSE GOES BY. Copyright © 2013 by Elizabeth J. Duncan. All rights reserved. Printed in the United States of America. For information, address St. Martin's Press, 175 Fifth Avenue, New York, N.Y. 10010.

www.thomasdunnebooks.com
www.minotaurbooks.com

Library of Congress Cataloging-in-Publication Data

Duncan, Elizabeth J.
    Never laugh as a hearse goes by : a Penny Brannigan mystery / Elizabeth J. Duncan.
        pp. cm.
    ISBN 978-1-250-00825-1 (hardcover)
    ISBN 978-1-250-02049-9 (e-book)
    1. Brannigan, Penny (Fictitious character)—Fiction.   2. Congresses and conventions—Fiction.   3. City and town life—Wales—Fiction.
4. Wales—Fiction.   I. Title.
    PR9199.4.D863N48 2013
    813'.6—dc23

                                                        2013025277

Minotaur books may be purchased for educational, business, or promotional use. For information on bulk purchases, please contact Macmillan Corporate and Premium Sales Department at 1-800-221-7945, extension 5442, or write specialmarkets@macmillan.com.

First Edition: November 2013

10   9   8   7   6   5   4   3   2   1

In loving memory of
Patricia and Ronald Mann

Acknowledgments

*T*his book was inspired by Carol Lloyd, a reader in California I have never met in person but have come to know through our correspondence.

About two books ago Carol mentioned Gladstone's Library, located in North East Wales not far from Chester. Wouldn't it be wonderful, she wrote, if one of your books could be set there. Perhaps Rev. Thomas Evans attends a conference . . .

So that's how this book came to be. Thank you, Carol, for suggesting I set a book in this stunningly beautiful building.

Thanks are due to the Library's warden, Peter Francis, for his support of this project and for ensuring my visits were comfortable and I had everything I needed. I enjoyed our conversations and the opportunity to do an evening presentation at the Library on the importance of setting in the crime novel. I hope I managed to capture the ambience and atmosphere of the Library in my novel. Gladstone's Library is the perfect destination for a writer, reader, student, or anyone seeking a quiet, well-appointed place to reflect, work, or think in a unique environment that blends belonging with history.

Also in Wales, thank you to Peter and Sylvia Jones for their interest and support of my writing. A chance encounter twice in one day has led to a valued friendship. And to PC Chris Jones for advice and information relating to the North Wales Police.

My thanks as usual to Carol Putt and Madeleine Matte for their input and to my agent, Dominick Abel, and editor, Toni Kirkpatrick. Special thanks to author Hannah Dennison for her friendly support, encouragement, and problem solving help in our weekly Skypes.

And finally, heartfelt thanks to Lucas Walker and Riley Wallbank, who take such good care of Dolly while I'm writing in Wales or attending conferences. I couldn't do it without you.

Never Laugh as a Hearse Goes By

One

*H*ello, darling. It's me. Just wanted to let you know that I will be attending the conference at the library after all. It'll be wonderful to see you, but we'll have to be careful. We wouldn't want . . . well, you know." The speaker cleared his throat and hesitated, as if trying to decide whether he should say anything more. Then, apparently deciding to leave it at that or perhaps just not wanting to say too much, he ended with a somewhat lame, "Right, well, bye now, and we'll talk soon, I hope."

Penny Brannigan's finger hovered over the delete key. Then, setting down a bag of shopping, she eased herself into the wingback chair beside the telephone, and when she was seated reached down and picked up a small cat who settled comfortably into her lap. She stroked his luxurious grey fur as she listened to the message again. She did not recognize the caller, and this voice-mail message, spoken in a precise, cultured English accent tinged with a bit of border Welsh, was clearly not meant for her. The man had misdialed and got a wrong number, her number. She pressed the Save button.

"Well, Harrison," she said. "What do you make of that?" Harrison purred loudly and kneaded her lap with his paws. "You don't care, do you? Of course you don't and why should you?" She put him down and with him weaving in and out of her legs she walked to the kitchen to see about meals for both of them.

"What do you want for your supper?" She opened a cupboard, pulled out a tin, and showed it to him. "Salmon?" Harrison meowed his approval.

"Very intriguing, indeed," agreed Victoria Hopkirk when Penny repeated the contents of the voice-mail message to her the next morning. "Who was the message meant for, I wonder? And as for being careful. . . ." She paused to listen as the sound of the front door opening announced the arrival of Rhian, the receptionist at the Llanelen Spa. A moment later Rhian poked her head into Victoria's office. "Good morning." She grinned at Penny and Victoria, who returned her greeting.

"Our first clients will be here any minute," said Rhian, directing a meaningful look at Penny. "We've got that wedding party booked in today, remember. Hair, waxing, massages, manicures, the works. They've all got to be sorted. You'll have to speak to them and decide who's getting what done and in what order, Penny."

Penny gave Rhian a brief nod, rose from her chair and

took a few steps toward the door and then turned to look at her business partner. "I might just ring the library today and see if they've got a conference coming up."

"A conference? Here? At our little library?" Victoria laughed. "There's barely room for the books, never mind a conference. Where would people sit? In the children's section? On those little plastic chairs?"

Penny threw her a dark look. "Don't forget you've got to sort out that appointment with the solicitor to start working out the licensing agreements for the hand cream." She closed Victoria's office door behind her and set off down the hall to the manicure room to prepare for her first client.

As the morning wore on her thoughts kept returning to the puzzling voice-mail message and she asked herself the same question Victoria had: Who had the message been meant for?

"I know you aren't exactly keen to go," said the Rev. Thomas Evans, "but my dear girl, you know what the bishop's like."

"No, I don't, actually," his wife replied. "And as I don't work for him, I don't see why I should have to go. And 'not exactly keen' is putting it mildly, I might add." She selected a piece of toast from the toast rack and made a great, noisy show of buttering it and slathering it with thick-cut orange marmalade. "And for four days, too." She bit off the corner of her toast and looked at him steadily while she chewed.

"Well, it's meant to be a get-together for the wives too, or should I say spouses? After all, we do have a couple of women rectors." The kindly rector mulled that over for a moment. "I'm sure even the word 'spouses' will cause offence to someone. 'Partner', then, although I detest that word, for some reason." He took a sip of coffee and let out a little sigh. "It's all so complicated nowadays." He folded his hands over his chest and gazed fondly at his wife. "Although what the partners are meant to be doing while the rest of us are attending to church business, I have no idea, but I'm sure something interesting will be organized for you." He brightened. "And apparently the food there is very good. Everything is homemade, and I hear the scones are especially delicious."

He got up from the table, walked round to his wife, bent over and put his arms around her shoulders. "Please, Bronwyn, love, I need you to do this for me. Couldn't you show just the tiniest bit of enthusiasm?"

She buried her face in the familiar comfort of his green cardigan. It smelled of old books with the faintest whiff of cigarette smoke.

"It's Robbie, isn't it?" The rector asked the question but knew the answer.

Bronwyn nodded into the wooly warmth. "I can't bear the thought of being away from him for so long," she wailed. "Four whole days."

"I know it seems like an eternity to be apart from him, but really, in the grand scheme of things, four days isn't so very long. And he'll be fine. Jones the vet's going to look after him and Robbie will get lots of attention, you know he will. Everyone at the practice loves Robbie. You could leave those special treats he likes so much with the staff to give him and we could see if Penny would look in on him."

Bronwyn sniffled into a tissue. "I suppose you think I've gone all soft and daft."

Sensing progress, the rector responded immediately with reassurance.

"Of course I don't think you're daft! I know how much he means to you and how much you love him." She gave him a sharp glance. "*We* love him," the rector hastily corrected himself.

Hearing a soft clicking sound coming down the hallway, Bronwyn jumped up from her chair. She bent down as a cairn terrier, eyes bright with anticipation, trotted into the dining room and jumped into her open arms.

She held him close, stroking his beige fur and murmuring, "Who's my darling boy, then?"

She held him for a few more minutes, glancing at the rector over the top of Robbie's head, then set him down.

"And speaking of Penny," said the rector, "Why don't you treat yourself to a manicure before the conference? Go on."

Bronwyn looked at her hands. They were lightly flecked with brown spots and the smooth contours of youth had been replaced by skin that was starting to loosen.

"Oh, I don't know about that."

The rector covered her hand with his and gave it a little squeeze.

"Oh, go on," he repeated. "When was the last time you had a manicure? Before Christmas, wasn't it?"

Bronwyn met his eyes and the two exchanged loving, knowing smiles. "That's better," said the rector as he returned to his place, opened his newspaper and began to scan the headlines. A few moments later he set it down and remarked to his wife, "Listen, what do you say we decide that we're going to make the most of this conference? After all, how often do we get to go away for four days, all expenses paid? I'm sure someone in the vet's office would agree to send you an e-mail every day to let you know how Robbie's doing and that will put your mind at ease so you can relax and enjoy yourself. This little break will be a good chance for you to catch up on your reading. The drive to Hawarden will be lovely this time of year and the venue is beautiful. St. Deiniol's as was. Now known as Gladstone's Library. Such an imposing name. I haven't been there for many years and I can't tell you how much I'm looking forward to going back.

"Oh, and Bronwyn, there's another very special reason why I'm looking forward to this. I had an e-mail last night from my old friend from university days, Graham Fletcher. You'll remember him. Well, he's just been appointed the new warden at Gladstone's Library. A very distinguished position it is, and he's wanted it ever since I've known him. It'll be wonderful to see him again and catch up."

"Graham. Graham Fletcher. Well, well. I haven't thought about him in ages," Bronwyn said. "I wonder if he still has that red hair?"

"It would be amazing if he did," replied Thomas, thinking of his own grey hair, "since we're all about the same age. It's so long ago now that we all did our undergraduate degrees together. Those were the days. Back when we were all young and beautiful." He rubbed his chin. "Then he went up to Oxford to take a master's degree and I had the great good fortune to marry you, although I always felt that he fancied you for himself." Bronwyn smiled and raised an eyebrow. Reassured, the rector picked up his newspaper and opened it. A moment later he made a little tutting sound.

"Oh, dear. What a terrible thing."

"What is it?"

"It says here a couple in Aberystwyth returned from holiday to find their garden had been stolen. Ninety-three feet of it! All the plants just dug up and gone." He read a bit more. "And the bench, too!" He shook his head. "What wicked times we live in. What's the world coming to, I ask myself." He took a sip of coffee. "I must give this some thought. Perhaps there's a sermon in it. Garden," he muttered. "Garden of Gethsemane?"

Two

Graham Fletcher closed the door of his new office on the first floor of Gladstone's Library and, his heart pounding, leaned his back against it. As his breathing slowed, the beginning of a nervous smile appeared at one corner of his mouth. The smile crept across his face as he took in the bare bookshelves. When his gaze reached the heavy, old-fashioned oak desk, a tentative lifting of the corners of his mouth had become a broad, self-satisfied grin. He made a fist with his right hand and pulled it through the air toward his body. Then, with long, graceful strides he crossed the room to reach the leaded window that overlooked the tidy garden at the rear of the building. He grasped the handle, pressed down to release the clasp, and pushed the window open. A gust of cold, damp air rushed in as his eyes swept the rain-soaked scene below him. Four large rectangular grey stones which could serve as seats stood at the corners of two intersecting walking paths. Each stone, now darkened by rain, was carved at one end with an English word and its Welsh translation at the other: LOVE/CARIAD, PEACE/HEDDWCH, TRUTH/GWIRIONEDD, and JUSTICE/CYFIAWNDER.

Where the paths crossed stood a limestone sculpture of a half-woman, half-tree creature entitled *Sophia,* from the Greek for *wisdom.* She wore a carved asymmetrical diaphanous gown that exposed one breast and barely concealed the other. In her right hand she held a branch of leaves and, instead of legs and feet, her lower half was made up of gracefully twisted tree roots.

Fletcher didn't care for the benches and loathed the statue; he considered the grouping unnecessary and much too modern for his taste, but he was more than happy to live with it for now. Once he had established himself, he would find new homes for all of it.

He closed the window, pulled out the desk chair, and slowly—savouring every delicious moment of the descent—lowered himself into it. He switched on the desk lamp and gazed around the room, empty now of all the personal possessions of his predecessor. Fletcher, who had been in this office many times when it belonged to another man, pictured the empty bookshelves groaning under the weight of his own precious books—books it had taken him a lifetime of learning to collect.

The rain hammered steadily against the leaded windows with their small square panes, but nothing could dampen Fletcher's spirits on this day. For Graham Fletcher was a happy man. At the age of fifty-six, at a time when several of his colleagues were starting to think about retirement, he'd achieved his heart's desire. He'd been appointed to the position he'd wanted for almost thirty years and believed he deserved. Granted, the wait had been long and agonizing. The previous holder of the position, a man of robust health, had made it clear he had no plans to retire, so Fletcher had had to be patient, smiling while he bided his time. Finally, he'd heard the news he had been waiting for. The elderly incumbent had developed pneumonia and was not expected to survive. Fletcher stayed up late that night, praying and polishing his curriculum vitae.

And a month later, all the formalities completed, the bishop had approved his appointment as the warden of Gladstone's Library. The position came with a house on the grounds, but he didn't care about that. He could always get a house.

It was the Library he loved—the red sandstone building itself, of course, with its ornate displays of late-Victorian Gothic design but more than that he loved everything the Library stood for. It was about liberal thinking, open-mindedness, contemplation of a different kind of future, innovation, eliminating barriers and boundaries. Oh, the possibilities were endless. He felt on the very edge of a brave, new intellectual and theological world in which anything and everything might happen. And he would be the man to lead the change.

His long, slender fingers caressed the recently polished surface of the desk as he glanced at the small stack of files in one corner left by his late predecessor. There would be plenty of time later for those. This morning he wanted to meet with the staff and discuss the next major event on the Library's calendar of special events and the first on his watch: a conference of officials, including the bishop himself, and rectors from the Church in Wales. Also attending would be his old friend from university days, Thomas Evans and his wife, Bronwyn. He'd had hopes for Bronwyn himself, back then, and had been heartbroken, for a while, when she'd chosen Thomas. He himself had never married. It would be good to see them both again and to be able to welcome them to the Library as its warden. Warden. He loved the very sound of the word. It was all he'd ever wanted and he'd only had to tell one lie to get it.

Three

Pamela Blaine's blue eyes followed her husband, the Very Rev. Michael Blaine, Bishop of Holywell, as he opened his wardrobe, took out two shirts, and laid them smoothly on the bed. He gave her a brief, emotionless glance, then turned his attention to his cufflink tray. He picked up a square silver one with an offset sapphire, examined it, then set it down.

"Don't you have anything better to do than stand there watching me?" he asked, his head lowered and his back to her.

She remained in the doorway and said nothing. The uncomfortable silence stretched on until the bishop broke it.

"Well, unlike some of us, apparently, I've got a busy morning ahead of me." He glanced at his watch. "Still got a lot of things to do to get ready for the conference. One of our guest speakers has cancelled, I'm told. But that's got nothing to do with you. If you want to make yourself useful, you could start sorting out my clothes for the conference. Day and evening. Business. One set of casual. Oh, and an extra shirt, just in case. You know. The usual. But don't pack them yet. I don't want them creased. I just want to make sure everything has been laundered and gathered up so I don't forget anything. And I'm still waiting to hear what you've arranged for the women's program. But leave them some spare time, too, for their own pursuits and to enjoy the Library itself. Conference goers don't like a crowded program."

Before his wife could respond, he strode toward the door. "I'll be in my office if you need me."

He paused at the door and glanced at her. "If you need help organizing the women's program, I suggest you contact Bronwyn Evans in Llanelen. She's always organizing one thing or another. Cooking classes for new mothers, coffee mornings to raise money for literacy programs in Africa, or a good old-fashioned jumble sale. Minty can give you her contact details."

"Do you really think we need a women's program?" his wife asked. "If they have to come at all, surely they can keep themselves amused for a day or two? And anyway, it isn't just women. There's a husband or two in the mix."

"I'd like to provide a little entertainment or activity of some kind for them," replied the bishop. "Shows we care and it doesn't matter about the gender."

"Couldn't your marvelously efficient Miss Russell sort it?"

"No. She's got enough on her plate at the moment so don't expect any help from her. Anyway, all you've got to do is arrange one small event for one morning for a dozen

14

or so people. Just a couple of hours. Really, Pamela, how hard can that be, even for you?" And then, like a righteous breeze, he brushed past her and was gone.

His wife shifted to one side to let him by, then, with a tightening of her lips, entered the room. She hated the cruelly condescending way he had said that. *Even for you.* She looked with distaste at the immaculately pressed white shirts that she herself had ironed. What's the point, she thought. Really, Pamela, what's the bloody point? By the time we get to the conference, his clothes will have creases in them just from being in the suitcase. Anyway, if it's not the way I packed the shirts, it'll be the ties I chose. Or that I packed ties in the first place. "Really, Pamela, what were you thinking? When was the last time you saw anyone wearing a tie?" He'll find fault with something. He always does.

She reached into her pocket for her mobile. No messages. Odd, that. She thought she would have heard from him by now. It wasn't like him not to call.

Four

$\mathcal{H}$ello, Bronwyn. How are you?" Penny smiled at the rector's wife and then bent over to give Robbie a pat. "Are we walking in the same direction?" she asked as she straightened up. "I'm just heading over to the supermarket to pick up a couple of sandwiches for lunch. Victoria and I should make our own lunches, I know, but somehow we just never get around to it. Too lazy, I guess."

"Or maybe you're too busy. Thomas and I eat most of our lunches at home, so that's never a problem for us," Bronwyn replied, "although we do like the occasional picnic when the weather's fine. Still, that's just lunch from home in a different setting." Bronwyn pointed across the swollen River Conwy that marked the edge of the town. "Robbie and I've just finished our walk and we're on our way home. We were over by the falls this morning. I love this time of year, with spring just getting started. There's that tiny hint of warmth in the air. The promise of better days to come."

"The promise of two months of solid rain, more like," replied Penny, and laughing, they fell into step as Robbie led the way. "I'll be ringing the Spa to make an appointment to get my nails done," Bronwyn remarked as they approached the town's cobblestone square.

"Oh, that's nice," said Penny. "For Easter, is it?"

"Well, yes, that, and Thomas and I are going away for a few days right after. Four days, actually. I'm worried about Robbie, but Thomas keeps telling me he'll be fine and I'm sure he will. I had wanted to ask you if you'd mind terribly looking after him, but I know how busy you are at the Spa, and then you've got your adorable new kitten, so this wouldn't be the right time for you. We arranged to board Robbie at Jones the vet. They'll take good care of him, I'm sure. It's just that . . ."

"You'll miss him so much," Penny said. "But the four days will go quickly, you'll see. And two of them are travel days so they don't really count. If you look at it that way, it's more like two days. Going somewhere nice?"

"Yes, we are, actually," Bronwyn replied. "Thomas has a conference to go to, and the wives, well, spouses, are invited. I say, *invited,* but it's been made very clear that we're expected to go so there's not much choice. I'm not sure what we're meant to be doing while the men, well, mostly men but there are one or two lady rectors, are busy discussing important church matters. The bishop's wife is arranging a program for us and she's asked me to help. I had rather hoped we'd just be left to our own devices and then everyone would meet up at dinner. I'm bringing some books that have been gathering dust on my night table, and I'd like to catch up on my reading. The venue will be perfect for that." She thought for a moment. "Bringing books to a library. Coals to Newcastle."

"So it's a conference for clergy, then, is it?" Penny asked.

"Well, yes, rectors and officials from the Church in Wales," said Bronwyn. "At first I wasn't too keen on going because of Robbie, but Thomas helped me see things in a different light. Once I understood how much it means to him, I was happy to support him. Funny how changing your attitude toward something can make a change for the better. Now I'm quite looking forward to the break. Thomas says the venue is beautiful and perfectly suited to this type of conference. He's been wanting to go back there for years."

"Oh, it sounds lovely," said Penny. "And where is it you're going?"

"Gladstone's Library. It used to be called St. Deiniol's, but the name was changed a few years ago to Gladstone's Library."

"Oh, I see," said Penny, her eyes widening. "A conference at the Library. Well, that's interesting. Gladstone's Library. That's in . . . where is it?"

"A town called Hawarden." She spelled it out. "But pronounced Harden. In North East Wales, near the border. Not far from Chester. The Library is a stunning example of late Victorian architecture."

"Oh, right. Come to think of it, I have heard of it. And when is it, exactly, this conference?"

"It's the Tuesday to Friday right after Easter. We're to arrive Tuesday afternoon and leave after breakfast on Friday."

Bronwyn thought for a moment and then touched her

friend's arm. "I wonder, Penny, if you would consider coming along and giving the ladies a sketching lesson? Perhaps we could sketch the building? I could see about getting the materials if you told us what would be needed. Or it doesn't have to be a sketching class. Maybe you could give a talk on Victorian stained glass. Or church art? You could do anything along those lines, with an artistic Victorian theme. It's just that the bishop's wife, Mrs. Blaine she's called, asked me to sort out the programming for the ladies. She gave me a lot of flannel about how she'd heard I was so good at organizing things and would really value my help . . . but never mind about all that. I'd take it as a great personal favour if you'd agree to do something for us. I know so few people who have the kind of creative talent you do."

"Now who's flannelling who?" Penny started to laugh and after a moment, Bronwyn joined in good-naturedly.

Penny had arrived in North Wales twenty-five years earlier as a young Canadian backpacker touring the British Isles. She'd fallen in love with the market town of Llanelen, and the one or two nights that she intended to stay had stretched into years as she'd made friends, started a small business, and contributed to the life of the community. She had a degree in fine arts from a distinguished Canadian university, and although she now earned a good living from her business investment in the Llanelen Spa, which she and Victoria had renovated and opened just before Christmas, her knowledge and appreciation of art had continued to grow over the years.

"How many women would there be?" she asked.

"Well, that's the thing. Why they're even bothering is beyond me. Let me see. Well, there's me, of course, and

Mrs. Blaine. Pamela, I believe she's called. She's married to the bishop. Oh, I already said that. And then there's the bishop's secretary, but whether she'd be free to attend our sessions, I don't know. I expect she'll be required to attend the work groups and take the minutes. Or maybe she'd be too busy scurrying around behind the scenes making sure everything is in order . . ." Bronwyn shrugged. "And then there'll be other rectors from the diocese. Two of the rectors are women. Whether their husbands would attend, I don't know. And if they did attend, would they join the wives' group or do you think they'd be excused and allowed to follow their own pursuits? It's all so complicated. Do you know, I'm not exactly sure who all is going. I'll have to check with Thomas and let you know. Will you be home this evening? I'll ring you."

The police station at Llandudno buzzed with the usual noise of police officers going about their business. Officers left the station and made their way to the car park at the back of the red brick building on Oxford Road as the desk sergeant dealt with a steady parade of visitors who came to register a complaint, comply with a bail condition, drop something off, or ask to see a specific officer.

In a temporary office overlooking the car park, Det. Chief Inspector Gareth Davies checked his e-mail and then reached for his telephone and called his sergeant. "Morning, Bethan. Would you come in here for a moment please?" A few minutes later Sgt. Bethan Morgan appeared in front of his desk.

"What's up, sir?"

"It's a conference at Gladstone's Library. Group of clergy from the Church in Wales. One of our colleagues from St. Asaph was supposed to give them a little talk on how they can better protect their churches against the rise in thefts of lead and copper. Now he's been reassigned to a priority investigation and the superintendent's asking if we can send someone. So I think this would be a good opportunity for you to practice your presentation skills . . ."

The ringing of his mobile telephone interrupted him. He glanced at the caller ID and gestured at Morgan to sit down. "It's Penny. You don't have to leave, just take a seat. Sorry, but I should just take this." He turned his attention to his mobile.

"Hello, you."

He listened for a few moments and nodded.

"Right. Love to. Sounds great. We'll sort the details out soon."

He smiled as he pressed the button to end the call.

"Well," he said to his sergeant, "what are the chances of that? Penny just asked me if I'd like to get away for a few days to Gladstone's Library at the same time as this conference is on and I agreed, so I'll do the presentation. We'll find something else to keep you busy while I'm gone."

Bethan stood up. She knew Davies had been trying for some time to find the right time and the right place to spend a few days on a break with Penny, but something always got in the way of their plans. But it struck her as odd that Penny had been the one to ask him to go away. The two had been seeing each other since last summer, but Bethan felt the relationship was tilted emotionally in Penny's favour—that Davies's strong feelings for her were not returned with the same intensity. She's just not that into him, was the way Bethan put it. Or maybe she's just holding back, for some reason. Oh well, nothing to do with her. Leave them to it and she hoped they'd enjoy themselves. There was always plenty to do around the station to keep her busy.

Five

"Well, Penny, and how are things going with that nice policeman of yours?"

"Very well, thank you, Mrs. Lloyd." Penny finished applying the top coat to her client's nails and sat back as her client held her hands out in front of her to examine them. Satisfied with the results, Mrs. Lloyd nodded.

"Now I'm only thinking about you, Penny. It's just that you're not getting any younger so I hope things are moving in the right direction there." She gave Penny a sly smile. "Will we have a wedding to look forward to this summer, I wonder?"

Penny did not rise to the bait. "Well, Mrs. Lloyd, you're done for this week," she said briskly. "I hope you'll enjoy your bridge game tonight. It's still on, I suppose?"

"Oh yes. It would be nice to get some decent cards for a

change. Or a decent partner who knows better than to trump my ace. Perhaps tonight my luck will change."

Penny saw her client out, then headed for Victoria's office. "I couldn't believe it," she exclaimed, throwing herself into a chair. "'A wedding to look forward to!' Honestly, that woman."

Victoria looked up from her computer. "Well, Penny, maybe it's just as well she brought it up. She does have a point, I think. Have you thought about how you're going to respond to Gareth when he asks you?"

"Asks me?"

"Yes, when he asks you to marry him. As he surely will."

Penny frowned. "Marry him? Do you know something I don't? Do you know that he's going to? Has he said something to you?"

"Well, you must know how he feels about you. It's pretty obvious to the rest of us that he worships the bones of you. He's besotted."

Penny ran her hands through her hair, leaving one side sticking up. "I know," she said softly. "I wish he didn't feel quite so strongly. I think we're fine as we are. I don't want things to change. We're in a good place."

Victoria tipped her head and raised an eyebrow. "Are both of you in a good place, though? Maybe you are and Gareth not so much. I get the feeling he'd like things to move forward. Relationships can't stay in one place forever. Not at the stage you're at, anyway. It has to be going somewhere. Leading to something."

Penny sighed. "But does it, though? I don't want to hurt him but I'm really not sure I have anything more to give." She met her friend's gaze.

"Do you love him?" Victoria asked. "Because if you don't by now, maybe you never will."

Penny said nothing as the silence between them grew thicker and heavier. She raised her shoulders a little and then sank back in her chair.

"I'm not sure what I feel for him. I want to love him. I find him very attractive and he's a wonderful, decent, kind man, but there's just something. Oh, I don't know. I don't know how to put it." Her voice trailed off and then she tried again. "I'm not sure what I'm supposed to feel at my age. I feel comfortable with him. I like talking to him. I like going out with him. I enjoy his companionship. He's fun to be with. But when I'm not with him I don't feel that aching longing, that intense need to be with him. So am I in love with him? Do I love him? I don't know. Maybe I do, but it's a different kind of love. It's not the grand passion we feel in our twenties or thirties; it's calmer and more settled."

She cupped her chin in her hand and thought for a moment.

"What I do know is that I don't want to marry him. That much I do know. And it isn't just him, I wouldn't want to marry anybody and to be honest, I don't think I ever will. I like my life as it is. I love the cottage. It's my home and for the first time in my life I've got everything just the way I want it. I don't want to share it with anyone and I don't want to move. But at the same time, I don't want to lose him."

Victoria let out a little sigh and nodded. "Well, hopefully you'll have a chance to sort things out while you're at the Library." Penny stood up.

"And you'll look after Harrison while I'm away?"

"Of course. I assume he's just like every other cat I've

ever known. Once he works out that I know how to use the can opener we'll get along just fine."

Victoria leaned back in her chair and looked at Penny's retreating back. She saw a slim woman in her early fifties who dressed well and took good care of herself. Her carefully shaped red hair, cut and coloured after hours in the Spa's hair dressing salon, was all one length and curved in neatly below her ears, almost reaching her shoulders.

I don't think that relationship is going in the right direction, Victoria thought, feeling anxious for Penny's happiness.

A few weeks earlier, Victoria had met a cello player in Florence and had got caught up in a passionate affair that ended abruptly when Victoria discovered he was married and still living with his wife. But she thought about him often and longed for him, or at least longed for the single man she'd thought he was and wished he'd been. Penny's got it wrong about there being no place for passion in a middle-aged romance, Victoria told herself with a small shrug. But everyone's different and maybe she and Gareth will find what works for them and settle for that, whatever it turns out to be.

With a sigh, she turned back to her computer and started printing off the documents she'd need to set up the meeting with the lawyer. A local woman, Dilys Hughes, had created a hand cream that promised extraordinary results. In her seventies, Dilys had the hands of a woman decades younger. The skin was taut with no blemishes or brown spots. She'd used the hand cream almost all her adult life and the results were impressive. Penny and Victoria wanted to sell it as a private-label product for their Spa, but first they had to get legal access to the formula. She had a feeling Dilys wasn't going to be easy to work with.

Six

*A*raminta Russell, the bishop's secretary, glanced up from her computer as her employer entered the large office suite they shared on the ground floor of the house where the bishop and his wife had lived since their marriage. Minty's white hair was all one length and fell to just below her ears from a centre part. Her glasses were rimless, and while trendy, gave her a curiously old-fashioned look as if she might have been the headmistress of an exclusive ladies' college in the 1930s. She wore a dark purple pleated skirt with a lavender twin set and a graceful three-strand pearl necklace that her mother had left her.

"Good morning, Bishop."

Blaine nodded as he strode past her into his office, indicating that she should follow him.

"Arrangements for the conference coming along well?"

he asked as he settled in his chair and reached for the papers Miss Russell had placed in his in-tray.

"Well, the North Wales Police have been very accommodating," she replied. "They're sending a replacement for the first officer who was supposed to speak to us and then got reassigned." She glanced at her notebook. "A DCI Gareth Davies will be speaking to the group so that seems in order."

Blaine nodded as he turned a page of the document he was scanning. "Good. Anything else?" He did not look up.

"No, I don't think so. I'm working on the overview of all the parish activities, and I'll have all the reports printed and ready for you in good time."

Blaine made no reply and kept reading, his chin resting on his hand.

"And then there's the speaker who is going to explain how we can use mobile telephones to bring in more donations," Minty said as she lifted a page of her steno book. "That speaker is lined up and ready to go. In fact, he seemed quite keen."

The bishop groaned.

"Well, that's the reality today," Miss Russell said. "Studies show that people would be happy to donate more if they could use modern technology to do so. Hardly anyone carries cash. And coins and bills are so tiresome to count after the service when the sidesmen just want to be off home to their Sunday lunches. So there's the convenience factor and if the new system would appeal to a younger congregation and bring in more money, then it would seem to be a very good thing. The way of the future."

The bishop made a noncommittal kind of unhappy,

whining noise and Miss Russell remained standing in the doorway but said nothing.

"Well?" he asked, finally raising his eyes to meet hers. "Is there something else?"

"Yes, sorry, there is one thing," Minty said. Blaine continued to maintain hard eye contact.

"Well, go on, then. What is it?"

Minty hesitated, looked away, and then said, "It's a personal matter. It's just that my sister is not well. She found a lump and they ran some tests and now she's scheduled for surgery. I wondered if I might have a few days with her. Her husband's next to useless; he can barely make a cup of tea, let alone put a decent meal together. It's a good job he works in a pub because that's where he'd be spending all his time anyway. Constance, that's my sister, she'll need help while she recovers. I'll just be gone for a few days before Easter and I'd arrange to be back Easter Monday to make sure everything's ready for the conference."

"Well, it can't be helped, I suppose," Blaine said with a frown. "Just make sure you're back in time for the conference and everything's nailed down and ready to go. No loose ends."

Miss Russell gave him a grateful smile. "Yes, Bishop. I will." She had wanted to ask him if she might have a few days off after the conference to spend with her sister but the timing didn't seem right to put it to him. She'd make sure the conference went off without a hitch, and then put in her request at the end of it when he was bound to be in a better mood. As her sister and brother-in-law lived in a small village a few miles from Hawarden, where Gladstone's Library

31

was located, it made sense to go to her sister directly after the conference had wrapped up. She might even be able to get a ride with her brother-in-law, Montel, who worked in the pub across the street from the Library.

"Right, well, I'll just put the kettle on. I expect you'd like a cup of tea." The bishop had returned to his reading and did not reply.

Hywel Stephens, the accountant who handled the church finances, was also thinking about the conference. Good looking in an obvious way, he was tall and kept himself in shape. He appreciated nice things and his taste showed in the fine cut of his suit, designer cologne, and expensive haircut. This morning he'd arrived early at his office, met with a couple of clients, sorted out a tax problem, and now had about an hour before lunch to work on the diocesan accounts. The bishop had asked him to present a financial report at the upcoming conference and he had to prepare for that. He wouldn't be attending the whole conference, but would join the group for lunch on the Wednesday and then walk the group through the financial situation in the afternoon session.

He called up a spread sheet and worked his way up and down the rows and columns of figures. Everything seemed in order. Like the curate's egg, it was good in parts. Some parishes were doing better than others but combined they were showing enough to cover operating costs with some left over to put a bit aside for a rainy day or, God forbid, a new roof. The bishop would be pleased about that, the accountant thought, and hopefully wouldn't ask too many questions. He tapped his keyboard to close the document.

Seven

*I*n the early evening of Easter Monday, the night before the conference, Minty let herself into the bishop's house. The office suite was separated from the rest of the house by a locked door and she moved about quietly, so as not to disturb the bishop and his wife. She could vaguely hear a television playing somewhere in the house. She knew the timing of her sister's illness had annoyed the bishop, who saw it as a personal inconvenience, but it could not be helped. Constance was recovering much more slowly than the doctors had predicted, and although Minty had desperately wanted to stay longer, she'd returned to get ready for the conference. She had assured the bishop she would and he expected nothing less.

She looked at the large stack of unopened mail that had been tossed on her desk and with a resigned sigh, reached for her letter opener. A single woman who needed to work, she had expected to retire at sixty as British women used to. But with the downturn in the economy, she was glad that the laws had been changed so she could continue on in the position she had held for almost ten years. Money was definitely an issue; she hadn't saved nearly enough for a comfortable retirement. And the cost of everything kept going up. She couldn't remember the last time she'd had a new winter coat. Vacations were spent with her sister or a cousin in Devon.

She enjoyed her job, most of the time, and her old-fashioned, unquestioning loyalty to her employer was almost absolute. But lately feelings of resentment had begun to creep in. She found it harder to get up in the morning to come to work. There were other things she'd rather be doing. She was more tired than she used to be at the end of the day and occasionally she longed for a nap after lunch. There were times when it took every ounce of restraint she had to not tell the bishop's spoiled, vain wife what she really thought of her. As for the bishop, although she was well aware of his flaws, she respected him. She admired his sharp, clear thinking and the way he made decisions quickly. He hated dithering. He was all about getting the job done quickly and efficiently. She knew that some thought him cold and even questioned his suitability for the role of bishop but she thought his first-rate administrative skills made him perfect for the job. He held people accountable. If he had one weakness, though, it was that he did not pay as close attention to the financials as he ought to. After all, they tell the real story and the only one that matters for any organization.

She reached out a veined and freckled hand to switch on

the desk lamp, and in the little pool of white light that flooded her desktop, she slit open the first envelope. Soon she had a small pile of parish reports to analyze, enter into a spreadsheet and summarize for the bishop's attention. She checked her watch. That late already! She was beginning to regret not taking an earlier train. She walked into the small kitchen that adjoined the office and filled the kettle. A cup of tea would help. It always did.

An hour later, puzzled, she sat back in her chair. She peered closer at the document on her computer screen and took a reflective sip of cold tea.

That's rather peculiar, she thought, running her finger along the rows of numbers that summarized various activities in the different parishes. In one parish a set of numbers was substantially higher than in the others. She compared the figures on each side of the parish that puzzled her. Perhaps there had been some kind of error. She double-checked her entry figures one last time and then gave up. She printed out the document, circled a number and tucked the paper in her handbag. She'd take a closer look in the morning. It was easier to make sense of numbers when they were on paper. It was late, she was tired, her eyes felt strained; at her age she much preferred working by daylight. She took off her glasses and rubbed her eyes. Just a few bills to pay and then she'd be off home. She didn't understand why the bishop was so resistant to the idea of using modern technology to process donations. She'd been paying the bills online for the bishop, his wife, and the diocese for ages and it saved a lot of time and bother. The old way of writing out cheques and putting them in the post belonged to another century. Pushing aside the thought of the small pile of unopened bills awaiting her at home, she picked up the last bill to be paid: Mrs. Blaine's mobile. She checked that the previous payment had been credited and then scanned the call list to make sure no incorrect charges had been listed.

She recognized one number that she had noticed on the bill over the past couple of months but was surprised at how many times it appeared on this one. That's odd, she thought. Why would she be calling him so often? In fact, why would she be calling him at all? A moment later she gave a little exclamation of understanding as she realized the implication. Mrs. Blaine having an affair? No, surely not. There must be some perfectly reasonable explanation. But what else could it mean? Minty covered her mouth and yawned as a wave of troubled fatigue washed over her. Too many numbers. Phone numbers. Parish numbers. Too much to think about. She was that tired, she wasn't thinking straight, was all. Time to pack up and get off home to the small rented flat she could barely afford above a ladies' dress shop. She made a mental note to start checking the newspaper advertisements when the conference was over to see if she could find cheaper accommodation. A cozy bedsit, maybe.

She checked her watch. If she left within the next five minutes she could just make the bus and, as it would be so late when she got home, she wouldn't have to worry about switching on the heat. Just as well, as the little jar in which she kept the pound coins to feed the meter was almost empty.

She tucked her notebook and a couple of pens in her handbag and checked her desk to see if there was anything else she'd need at the conference. She wished the bishop had invited her to travel to Hawarden with him and his wife, but he had not mentioned it.

She would take the train to Chester in the morning and make her way from there to the Library on the number 4 bus. She'd have to pack light so getting on and off the bus would not require too much effort. It might be a good idea to arrive a little early to have a word with the bishop about those numbers on the spreadsheet. Something wasn't right and the bishop should know so he would be up to speed before Mr. Stephens, the accountant, did his presentation. He might also want to discuss their meaning with the accountant.

And then there was the little matter of the telephone number that appeared so often on Mrs. Blaine's statement. She had an idea what it meant, but she wasn't sure what to do about it. Probably best to do or say nothing. None of her business if Mrs. Blaine was seeing a fancy man, but the bishop might want to know about it. But would telling the bishop be an example of her loyalty or would it just hurt him needlessly? And what if she told him and it turned out she'd got hold of the wrong end of the stick and his wife was not having an affair at all? What if there was a perfectly reasonable explanation for the phone calls, even though Minty couldn't, for the life of her, imagine what that might be.

Oh, she thought, switching off her desk lamp, it was all just too much to think about. She wasn't paid enough to have to deal with all these problems.

Eight

Pulling her wheeled suitcase behind her, Minty bumped her way across the forecourt of Chester railway station. After a quick glance at the taxi cabs waiting to pick up fares, she crossed the street and walked to the bus stop. The bishop had told her to take a taxi from the station, but she'd take the bus now and later she would cobble together something that looked like a taxi receipt.

As the bus wound its way through the narrow streets of the English walled town, dropping off passengers in front of shops with colourful window displays, Minty gazed through the mud-spattered window, envying the bustling shoppers. The town centre gradually gave way to suburbs and then countryside, so she settled back in her seat and closed her eyes, thinking about the long list of tasks still on her to do list. She opened her eyes when the driver announced they were approaching Hawarden.

Located six miles from Chester, the town of Hawarden, just inside the Welsh border, is best known for its long ties with the family of William Ewart Gladstone, who served as Britain's prime minister a record four different times in the second half of the nineteenth century. A champion of liberalism, rights for women, and education over his long and distinguished career, he was also a great reader who owned some 32,000 or so books that he decided not to bequeath to his alma mater, the University of Oxford, on the grounds that that distinguished university already had enough books.

The idea of creating a different kind of library appealed to Gladstone. A residential library that was private, because it received no public funding, yet open to everyone. Before his death in 1898 he transferred his books, many of which contain annotations in his own hand, to a temporary building, known as the tin tabernacle. After his death, a permanent, much grander building was built to house the collection. This building, completed in 1906, comprised the library and a residential facility for students, staff, and visitors. It remains today the only prime ministerial library in Britain.

Built of red sandstone with an exuberance of stylized Victorian detailing, the two-storey Library features dormers, gables, and plenty of Gothic touches. There are oriel windows, pointed doorways, leaded pane windows, and pinnacles and small statues of great thinkers, such as Aristotle, in canopied niches.

Minty struggled off the bus at the stop closest to the Library entrance, crossed the street, and strolled along the pavement past the curving stone wall covered in greenery to the Library entrance. She paused for a moment on the lichen-covered path to take in the extravagant statue dedicated to the memory of the Library's namesake, William Gladstone. She continued on her way, and as she reached the main entrance a young staff person opened the door for her and helped her in with her bag.

Minty paused in the reception area to look around. She had grown up in the area, and although she had been to the Library many times it always filled her with a sense of quiet, respectful awe. She loved it more on every visit and, in fact, it was she who had suggested holding the conference here. Sometimes it reminded her of an elite college and at other times of an understated boutique hotel. But it always reminded her of a much loved and much used country house with its quiet comforts and atmosphere of tranquil exclusivity. However, as she wandered down the hallway, glancing at the leaflets on the deep-set oak windowsills, she was reminded that first and foremost, it is a library—a place for research, reading, and learning—at once traditional and modern. Pamphlets offered week-long courses in beginners Latin, Greek, Hebrew, or Welsh and promoted presentations by visiting authors. Several courses focused on the Victorians and others connected theology and film—a three-day course exploring the cultural context of Jesus at the Movies looked interesting.

There was nothing announcing upcoming conferences, such as the one she herself had organized, as these events were private.

After asking a staff member if the bishop and his wife had arrived and being told they had not, she went upstairs to her room to get settled in, review the conference arrangements, and lie down for an hour or so before the evening welcome reception began in the Gladstone Room. She took out the sheet of figures she had printed off the night before and, sitting on the edge of her bed, mulled them over. The discrepancy in the one parish bothered her. There was increased activity, but as far as she could tell not the corresponding increase in revenue she would have expected to see. Wondering if she should take it upon herself to ask Hywel Stephens, the accountant, about that, she pulled the puffy white duvet over her, closed her eyes and drifted blissfully into a much longed for nap.

An hour later, somewhat refreshed but a little groggy, she splashed some cold water on her face and then checked her to do list. The warden! She must speak to him about an important last-minute request from the bishop before the reception started. She hurried down the hall in the direction of his office. She opened the door that separated the bedroom wing and entered the open space at the top of the stairs. As she did so, the door to the warden's office opened and a couple emerged, followed by the warden himself.

"Wonderful to see both of you again," Graham Fletcher said to the departing couple, "and we'll catch up some more at the reception, I'm sure. I hope you enjoy the conference. Do let me know if there's anything I can do to make your stay here at the Library more comfortable."

With smiles all round, the couple left and he ushered Minty into his office.

"Might I just go over a few last minute details with you, Warden?" she asked. "The bishop wants me to make sure everything goes smoothly."

As Thomas and Bronwyn strolled down the green-carpeted hall to their bedroom after their short meeting with their old friend, Bronwyn looked at her husband.

"Didn't he look exactly like the cat that got the cream?" she said. "I've never seen a man so pleased with himself." "He may have got the cream," Thomas replied, slipping his arm around his wife's waist and pulling her closer to him, "but I was the lucky one. I got you."

Nine

"*B*ishop, I wonder if I might have a word?"

The bishop sighed and raised a hand to his temple. "Not a good time, Minty," he said, glancing at the document in her hand. "Pamela and I arrived later than I wanted to and our guests are about to arrive. I'll need to circulate. I'm sure it's important, but whatever it is you want to tell me, it'll have to wait." He gestured at the paper. "We can discuss that later. There'll be plenty of time."

"Yes, of course. It's just that . . ."

"My wife will be down in a minute, so if you wouldn't mind just making sure everything is under control until she gets here," the bishop interrupted, eyeing the door. "Oh, look, there's, er . . ."

"Oh, that's Reverend Thomas Evans and his wife,

Bronwyn. From Llanelen," Minty supplied helpfully, after glancing at the doorway. "I saw them a few minutes ago coming out of the Warden's office."

"Yes, of course it is." The bishop stepped forward.

"Thomas," the smiling bishop said in the warmest voice he could muster, extending his hand. "And Bronwyn, do, please, come right in. Welcome. How nice it is to see you. So glad you could make it. How are things in Llanelen? Well, I hope. Still busy with the coffee mornings? The others will be here in a moment, I'm sure."

And then, in the way of social events, the Gladstone Room suddenly seemed filled with people and the polite buzz of party chatter. Introductions were made, hands were shaken, kisses were given and received, old acquaintanceships were renewed, and news and gossip exchanged. But genuine smiles were rare and faded quickly and after the initial greetings, silences hung heavy, and what conversation there was seemed forced. The atmosphere seemed charged with reluctance and formality as if everyone found it all rather heavy going and could think of lots of other places they'd rather be and things they'd rather be doing.

A Library staff member passed amongst them, offering glasses of wine, followed by another server who held a tray of elegant canapés. Minty circulated from little group to little group, making introductions where necessary and exchanging a pleasant word or two with everyone.

"Ah, Miss Russell, have you met my wife, Bronwyn?" Thomas Evans introduced the two women, who smiled at each other.

"No, I don't think I have. So nice," Minty said. "I know Reverend Evans from his name on the Llanelen records

46

and reports, of course. Mind you, I haven't been to Llanelen in years. Is the tea shop still there, just beside the bridge? Lovely scones, as I recall."

As Bronwyn was about to reply, the conversation level dropped and died away as two men entered the room. All heads turned toward them. One, a tall man in his early sixties with thinning grey hair that looked as if it had missed its shampoo date two or three days ago and wearing a clerical collar, looked around the room with cheerful confidence bordering on arrogance. The heavyset man by his side seemed much younger.

"Oh no, he hasn't," muttered Minty. "I distinctly informed Reverend Shipton that the bishop had forbidden him to bring his, er, friend. Companion. Partner. Whatever." The bishop, who was deeper down the room toward the fireplace, looked up from his conversation with Warden Graham Fletcher and seeing the two men, broke off abruptly and walked toward them. A small cluster of throbbing veins appeared at his left temple.

"Reverend Shipton," he said with an arctic edge to his voice.

The taller of the two men smiled at him. "Yes, good evening, Bishop, and I'd like to introduce my partner." He grinned at the man standing next to him. "This is Azumi Odogwu." Mr. Odogwu smiled shyly at the bishop, revealing very large, gleaming white teeth set in a shiny, very dark face.

The bishop did not offer to shake hands. He turned and looked around the crowd until he saw who he was looking for, standing beside Thomas and Bronwyn.

"I did tell him, Bishop," Minty said in a low voice a few moments later. "I made it very clear that it was compulsory that he attend but that you had forbidden his male partner to accompany him. I told him his partner would not be welcome." The bishop scowled.

"Well, Minty, you will just have to tell him again and this time, in a way that leaves no doubt I mean what I say and that I expect him to respect my wishes." He reached into the inside pocket of his jacket. "And now I must make my welcoming speech."

"Oh, but tell him now . . . in front of all these people? I don't think I would feel comfortable doing that, Bishop. Could we not wait until after the reception and then I could have a quiet word with him? Do you not think that would be much better? We wouldn't want to make a scene and spoil the occasion for everyone else. The conference is just getting started."

"Very well. But his friend is not to spend the night here." Minty could hear the quotation marks framing the word *friend*. "That would be unthinkable. And make sure Nigel Shipton has been assigned a single room. Single, if you understand my meaning."

He strode off and resumed his position in front of the fireplace, commanding the room. All eyes turned toward him and everyone listened attentively as he made his opening remarks.

When he had finished, Bronwyn gave Minty a kind, sympathetic look. "If you'd like, Miss Russell, I'd be glad to help you find the right phrases to use for this unpleasant task. I borrowed a magazine recently from the library and there was an article in it on how to defuse a difficult situation with thoughtful words. How you can say what you need to say tactfully and kindly, without harshness or in a way that could cause hurt."

"Please, Bronwyn, do call me Minty. And yes, I'd be very interested in hearing what the article had to say." She smiled gratefully and as the party chatter resumed around them, a server approached carrying a tray. She lowered it so the little group could examine its contents.

"Oh, yes please. Prawns!" said Bronwyn. "I love them. How about you, Minty? Will you have one?"

Minty shook her head and held up her hands, waving them slightly.

"No, I couldn't possibly. I have the most dreadful allergy to shellfish. All seafood. Even just a bite of one of those prawns would make me terribly ill. I have to be very careful."

"Oh, I'm so sorry to hear that," said Bronwyn, helping herself to a prawn mounted on a little stick with a cherry tomato where its head used to be. "A cousin of mine had an allergy to nuts and what a nuisance it was. She carried a device around with her so she could give herself an injection in case she should accidentally be exposed to nut oil, which is apparently more common than you might think. Do you have such a thing?"

"It's called an EpiPen," said Minty. "It delivers a dose of epinephrine. And yes, I have one, and I always make sure it's in date." She patted the worn brown handbag slung over her shoulder. "I wouldn't dream of going anywhere without it. I've had to use it once or twice and I believe it saved my life."

She glanced around the room. The small reception was beginning to thin out but Reverend Shipton and Mr. Odogwu were still there.

"Well, I'd better have a word with them before they escape," Minty said to Bronwyn in a low voice. "You know, everything about this beautiful building speaks to forward thinking, inclusion, tolerance and liberal values. The irony of what I am about to do is not lost on me."

Thomas and Bronwyn watched as she made her way to the two men, one tall, one short, one white, one black.

As the concerned couple exchanged sympathetic glances, Thomas muttered something. "Sorry, dear, I didn't quite catch that."

"I said, 'Talk about sending a boy to do a man's job.'"

"What do you mean?"

"I mean I probably shouldn't say what I really think about the bishop sending his secretary to speak to them, but the words 'dirty work' and 'cowardly' come to mind. Minty strikes me as a wonderfully competent woman and he's very lucky to have her."

With her back to the Evanses, Minty continued her conversation with the two men. Her tensed shoulders were raised slightly and occasionally she raised a hand, palm outstretched, in what looked like a pleading gesture. Reverend Shipton glared at her, and his companion looked up at him with a worried frown and then back to Minty.

A few moments later the two men left the room. Minty watched them go and then returned to the Evanses. She glanced at her watch and then gave the couple a wan smile, accompanied by a small shrug. They exchanged a few words and she moved on. A few minutes later she was chatting with the warden, who was circulating with a tray picking up abandoned glasses and napkins.

Bronwyn linked her arm through her husband's. "Well,

I guess that's all the excitement for now. Let's go up to our room. I fancy a bit of a lie down before dinner. This wine has made me a little sleepy."

"Not too sleepy, I hope," said her husband, giving her a big smile and a little squeeze.

Minty watched the last of the guests depart. When the room had emptied, she sat in a comfy wing chair and reached for her handbag which she had set down on a side table before tackling the unpleasant task of speaking to Reverend Shipton. She took out the document she had wanted to discuss with the bishop and looked over the numbers again. She looked in his direction, then folded the paper and thoughtfully replaced it in her bag.

On second thought, maybe the bishop wasn't the right person to discuss those numbers with. Maybe the rector of a certain parish would be far more interested in them. She tipped her head to one side. And maybe a quiet word with Pamela Blaine, the bishop's wife, might be a good idea, too. She felt the glimmer of a daring idea beginning to form.

"Oh, look, there's Penny and Gareth." Walking down the long front corridor that led from the dining room and the Gladstone Room at one end, to the vast library chamber itself at the other, with the reception area about halfway between, Bronwyn and Thomas caught sight of Penny and Davies in the reception area and waved to them.

"Hello, Penny," Bronwyn said as the two men shook hands and the four greeted one another warmly. "Just arriving are you? Did you have a good journey? You probably haven't had much of a chance to see anything, but isn't this place stunning?

"Very beautiful indeed," agreed Penny.

"Well, we'll leave you to get settled in. We were just going up to our room to get ready for dinner. There's already been a bit of a set to," Bronwyn said in a low voice as the four moved toward the green-carpeted staircase. "We're just coming from the opening reception. The bishop was simply furious that one of the rectors, Reverend Shipton, brought his partner with him. A young man from Nigeria, I heard someone say." Gareth Davies raised his eyebrows and managed to suppress a knowing smile.

Thomas Evans nodded at him but said nothing. "Oh dear me, yes, you can imagine how that went down," Bronwyn continued. "The secretary, Miss Russell, Minty is her first name, had the unpleasant task of telling them that Mr. Odogwu, that's the man from Nigeria, must not stay the night. I don't think Shipton liked it one bit and how the poor fellow will get back to Abergele, if that's where he lives, I have no idea. Shipton's from Abergele, He, of course, has no choice but to stay. If he wants to keep his job, that is." She looked to her husband. "Isn't that right, Thomas?" He nodded again.

"Well, we would have asked if you'd like to join us for a drink but if you're just coming from the reception you're probably not really in the mood. I expect you had something to drink at the reception. But I hope we'll see you at dinner," said Penny.

"Yes, that would be lovely," said Bronwyn. "It would be very nice if the four of us could sit together, but I'm afraid we can't. It would look rather odd if we didn't join the rest of the party." She shrugged. "At least for this evening. You know how it is on the first night."

"Of course. We'll see you soon. Perhaps after dinner we can discuss the presentation for the morning. The Robinson Room at 10, is it?"

At 6:45 P.M. Penny and Davies joined the queue just inside the dining room area. The menu for the evening meal, with three choices including a vegetarian option, was written on a white board and, after taking a few moments to decide what they wanted, guests approached the servery counter where friendly staff served meals cafeteria style. Guests then carried their trays through to the dining room, stopping to pick up cutlery and napkins before choosing where to sit.

Several square tables closest to the windows that over-looked the garden at the rear of the building had been pushed together to form one long, rectangular table that was to be occupied by members of the clerical party. The bishop, his wife, and Minty Russell sat together at one end of the table. A few moments later Bronwyn and Thomas entered the dining room and seeing empty spaces at the long table, walked slowly over to it, balancing their trays. Within a few minutes all the spaces at the table filled and everyone fell silent as the bishop rose to say a few words.

Penny and Davies, who entered the dining room just as the bishop finished saying grace, chose a round table off to the side of the room where they were fairly private but could still see everything.

"I wonder if Mr. Odogwu has gone home," Penny re-marked as Gareth filled her water glass.

"Possibly," he said. "Or heaven forbid, they've disobeyed the bishop's orders and he's having a lonely ham sandwich on his own in his room." He was seated facing the party so just had to shift slightly in his chair to see them. "That must be Shipton, the one sitting by himself at the end of the table. It's probably killing him to sit at the same table as the bishop. He can't seem to bring himself to have anything to do with any of them."

Penny turned her head sideways and leaned slightly forward. Shipton's thin, serious face seemed flushed with barely hidden anger or frustration as he took a vague swipe at wild wisps of grey hair carelessly arranged in a half-hearted, reluctant comb-over. His dark rimmed glasses were held in place by a black cord looped over the back of his neck. He took a sip of water and turned to Thomas Evans on his left and tipped his head as if listening. He then nodded vaguely and looked off into the distance. His eyes came to rest on Penny and she turned awkwardly back to look at Gareth. Their eyes met and each gave a little nod. They were thinking the same thing about Mr. Odogwu's motives for being in a relationship with Shipton—but neither wanted to say it out loud. Anyway, there was no need to. So Penny moved their thinking on.

"We've got our presentations in the morning and perhaps after lunch we could spend some time in the library and then go for a walk in the afternoon. Do a little exploring."

Davies slid his hand across the table and rested it lightly on top of Penny's.

"Yes, I'd like that. As for this evening, Bethan will be sending me some updated statistics that I'll need for my paper. But we could have coffee in the lounge with the others after dinner. Or maybe check out the Library."

"I think I'd rather wait and see it in daylight. I've heard it's quite magnificent and I really want to see it at its best."

Davies nodded and then checked his watch. "The presentation shouldn't take me too long to finish." He smiled at her. "I'm so glad we decided to come here. Are you? It's just the break we needed. Give us both the chance to relax a bit and spend some time together. It's a bit early to tell, I know, but are you enjoying yourself?"

Penny smiled back at him. She hoped it was the break they needed but she wondered if coming here had been the right thing to do. Something was starting to whisper to her that it was all going to end in tears for her, just as it was bound to for Reverend Shipton. It certainly wasn't his good looks and charm that the young, handsome black man found so appealing. It was more likely the burgundy European Union passport that the rector kept in his office drawer, and the bountiful benefits that flowed from it.

The walls of the dining room were decorated with framed covers from vintage Penguin paperback books with their distinctive colors: green and white for crime fiction or orange and white for general fiction. As she gazed at the covers a green and white one caught her attention and smiling, she pointed it out to Davies.

The Body in the Library, by Agatha Christie.

Davies smiled back. "Oh, God, I hope not."

Ten

Minty Russell was new to this, but you had to start somewhere and really, how hard could it be? Lots of people had done it and the only ones you ever heard about were the ones who got caught. She, Minty, was in possession of sensitive information that a certain lady would wish withheld from her husband, who held a prominent position, and therefore that lady would be more than willing to pay Minty for her silence. Yes, that was it. Miss Russell would think of it as confidential services. Discretion assured! Secrets kept! That other word, the one that started with *B*, was so unsavoury. She would think of Mrs. Blaine as her client. Victim is such a negatively charged word with unfortunate connotations. After all, agreeing to the arrangement would be Mrs. Blaine's choice, so where's the victimization in that?

She leaned back in the comfortable chair, slipped off her patent leather shoes with the bows on the toes, and rubbed her feet together. She smiled to herself as she reached into her handbag for the small bottles of vodka and orange juice she had brought with her.

She poured a generous splash of vodka into the glass, topped it up with juice, and reached for her steno notebook. The little business venture she had in mind was, technically, a crime, so she'd have to think everything through very carefully—and there was not much time. She marveled at her bold thinking. A few months ago she would never have even thought of something as audacious as this. But something in the way the bishop had been speaking to her recently had pushed her to the brink. Did she really owe any loyalty to someone who spoke to her like that? Who was so dismissive of everything she did to help him? Who took her for granted?

But what if she were caught? She took a sip and thought about that for a moment. And then a slow smile teased the corner of her mouth. It was most unlikely that Mrs. Blaine would report her to the police or tell her husband. And just suppose she were to have other clients. In the worst case scenario, they would report her to the bishop. And it wouldn't matter if they did.

You'd think a bishop would be the first person to go to the authorities if he discovered something as illegal as well, blackmail, going on right under his nose, Minty thought, but actually, the opposite would be true. He would not want the terrible stench of scandal spreading through his bishopric. He would not want to have to explain to the archbishop how something like this could have happened on his watch.

And a man in his position would most certainly not want his good name dragged through the sordid headlines of the red top press. When the media had finished their feeding frenzy, his career would be ruined beyond redemption.

Feeling confident and reassured, Minty moved on to mulling over the logistics of how to execute her plan.

How could she approach Mrs. Blaine without her husband knowing? Could she catch her for a few moments tomorrow morning, perhaps? Before that artist woman, Penny Brannigan, spoke? Yes, that might work.

Now, as to the amount. Fortunately, she managed the couple's personal accounts and knew exactly how much per month Mrs. Blaine could spare without her husband noticing. Of course, she would have to cut back here and there on the housekeeping to meet Minty's demands, but Minty had no doubt her client would find a way. Cooked properly, cheaper cuts of meat can be every bit as tasty as the expensive joints the Blaines enjoyed once or twice a week.

She took a small sip of her drink. And then there was the creative financial business in Reverend Shipton's parish. Definitely something dodgy going on there that he wouldn't want the bishop to know about. The accountant was meant to arrive late morning, join them for lunch, and then give his presentation on the church finances. She'd find the right moment for a quiet word with Nigel Shipton and the accountant on some pretext or other, and if her suspicions were right, she could very well have two more clients before the day was out!

But why stop at three?

There was also the not-so-small matter of Graham Fletcher and his academic credentials. Or, to be precise, his lack of academic credentials. The bishop had asked her to check Reverend Fletcher's curriculum vitae as a formality so he could approve his appointment, and Minty had done her due diligence. Reverend Fletcher had completed most of the requirements for a Master's degree in divinity from Oxford but there was the inconvenient loose end of an incomplete thesis. So close, Reverend Fletcher, but not quite there. Really, an ambitious man with his aspirations should have known better, Minty thought. You just don't expect that kind of deception from a man in his position, or at least the position he fancied himself in. And such an exemplary career in all other respects. Still, for some reason she didn't understand at the time, she'd decided to tell the bishop everything was in order. Perhaps subconsciously she'd thought this information might come in useful one day . . . give her some power over Reverend Fletcher, a favour she might call in when the time was right and the stakes were high enough.

Oh, this is deliciously easy, she thought. Why hadn't she thought of this simple scheme years ago? She needed more money herself just to have some kind of decent life and soon, to fund a comfortable retirement. And the extra money coming in would go a long way to helping her sister recover from her cancer operation. She might even be able to afford for her to go private, to get better care. Or hire a private nurse to look after her as she convalesced. And perhaps when Constance was recovered they might arrange a foreign holiday to someplace truly exotic. Not one of those cheap fortnights in Spain, all in, kind of thing. No, some place truly wonderful and unforgettably exotic . . . Istanbul or the Far East, perhaps. Just the two of them. It would all be so much better without her awful brother-in-law trailing along, drinking too much, complaining all day long about the heat and finding endless fault with the food and accommodation. Easing her sister's burden was a good enough reason right there, she told herself. In the meantime, she'd at least be able to pay for someone to come in and do the cooking and cleaning until her sister was back on her feet.

Minty looked at her own feet. She had always fancied a pair of those expensive shoes with the red soles that all the celebrities wore and if all went according to plan, it wouldn't be long before she could afford a pair. She laughed lightly. What would the bishop say if she turned up for work one morning in a pair of those? She laughed a little more at the very thought of it. And then she realized he would probably take no notice. But at the very least she could treat herself to a nice new brown leather handbag. Or maybe two. Black goes with just about everything.

She poured herself another drink, and made it a little stronger this time. She was excited and elated; sleep wouldn't come easy.

Eleven

The next morning after breakfast the conference goers divided into two groups, with church officials heading to the Anwyl Room, a small conference room on the ground floor beside the Gladstone Room, where the opening reception had been held the night before. The spouses went upstairs to the book-lined Robinson Room where Minty and the bishop's wife, who had arrived a few minutes early to check the room, were waiting to welcome them.

"Do you have everything you need?" Minty asked Penny as the women filed into the room.

"Yes, I think so," said Penny. "I've got a few handouts and samples here. I won't need the projector or anything like that. I'm all very low tech, me."

When the last of the participants was seated, Mrs. Blaine stepped out into the hall and Minty turned to Penny and said, "Oh, I almost forgot. The bishop has requested that you join us at the main table for lunch." As Penny bent over her notes, Minty straightened a few books on the bookshelves behind the door before following the bishop's wife into the hall, closing the door behind her.

"Would you mind if we kept the door open?" Bronwyn asked Penny. "I love the natural light and it seems a shame to shut it out."

"No, of course not," said Penny. "And aren't the other two joining us? I'll see what they're up to." She opened the door and stuck her head out. The corridor outside the Robinson Room led to the bedrooms to her left and behind the closed door on her right, to the staircase to the ground floor. The warden's office was located at the far end of the corridor, on the other side of the staircase.

A row of leaded windows with deep-set sills overlooking the Gladstone statue at the front of the building let in warm light that cast window-shaped patterns along the green-carpeted corridor. Pamela Blaine and Minty Russell, who were speaking in low tones as they leaned against a windowsill a little way down from the Robinson Room, seemed startled to see her and immediately turned and disappeared down the staircase. Penny returned to the room where the women were waiting for her presentation to begin.

"That's odd," she said to Bronwyn. "I thought they'd be joining us but they've disappeared. I guess they've got better things to do."

"Well, never mind. I'm sure Minty has loads of arrangements to see to. It's all go when you're in charge of a conference. So much to do behind the scenes." Bronwyn looked cheerfully around the room at the dozen or so women seated at table. "But we're all keen to hear your presentation, aren't we?" The women murmured agreement and Penny began discussing the life and work of Owen Jones, an influential Welsh architect and textile designer. English born, he was a founder of what is now the Victoria and Albert Museum in London and, Penny thought appropriately for the Library setting, his work was hugely influenced by the art and ornament of the Islamic world.

Forty-five minutes later, the women murmured words of thanks to Penny as they trooped out. "Well, I think that went pretty well," she said to Bronwyn as she packed up her samples and patterns. "Was it what you expected? Do you think they enjoyed it? I tried to keep it interesting and light, but honestly, this whole idea of doing a presentation for the few women here seems a bit daft. I wonder what the point of it was."

Bronwyn laughed and raised her hands. "Don't look at me."

"Well, we have some time to spare before lunch. Should we go to the Library? I've been dying to see it."

"I think I'll wait and see it with Thomas, if you don't mind, Penny. But you go on ahead."

"Right, then," said the bishop when the rectors were seated around the table in the Anwyl Room. "As you know, over the past few years we have been experiencing a huge increase in theft in our rural churches, from Bangor to St. Asaph and every place in between to right here in Hawarden. And this scourge is not just happening to us in Wales—this epidemic is sweeping right across the British Isles. So joining us this morning to advise us on what we can do in our own parishes to combat this theft and thuggery is," he glanced down at the card Minty had given him, "is Detective Chief Inspector Gareth Davies of the North Wales Police Service." The bishop made a small gesture in Davies's direction. "I'll turn it over now to DCI Davies."

"Good morning." Davies smiled at the earnest, sincere faces gazing at him. "I was delighted to be given the chance to speak to you today about an epidemic that concerns every one of us. Because it isn't only churches being stripped of their valuable metals—war memorials have been defaced for their metal and worryingly, copper wiring is being ripped out of electrical substations. And recently, we had a situation in which idiotic vandals actually tried to burn down a telegraph pole so they could steal the wiring attached to it. And all the damage these mindless vandals are doing takes a huge toll on the public purse. They will do whatever kind of destruction it takes to steal a few hundred pounds worth of materials. And then it takes thousands of pounds to repair the damage they caused. Not to mention putting lives at risk when metals are stolen from, say, railway lines.

"But we're here to focus specifically on the theft of precious metals from churches, what you can do to prevent it, and what the police are doing about the problem."

An hour later, Davies began to wrap up.

"So we've asked all scrap metal merchants to alert us to anything suspicious and we ask you to be vigilant and join your Neighbourhood Watch. And sadly, of course, it is no longer safe to leave your churches unlocked." The room was still, the only sound the soft scratching of Minty Russell's pencil as she took notes in her steno notebook. When Davies paused to meet the eyes of his audience, Minty's pencil remained poised over the page. "I know you want your churches to be places of quiet reflection, where anyone may find refuge for a few moments of prayer or contemplation, but we no longer live in a world where that's possible. You may, of course, have open hours at specific times, but to deter theft and vandalism, you must have a church official present and visible when the church is open."

Davies answered a few questions and handed out leaflets. After the bishop thanked him and invited him to join his table at lunch, the group broke for morning coffee in the Gladstone Room next door, where the warden was waiting to receive them. Davies spoke to him briefly but was interrupted by the apologetic arrival of Minty Russell.

"I'm so sorry to take you away, Warden," she said, "but I wonder if I might have a word. It's rather important, I'm afraid." She smiled at Davies, and the two moved to an empty corner of the room where she and the warden were soon deep in conversation. Davies watched them for a moment and then, just as he turned to set down his empty coffee cup and saucer, he noticed Minty hand the warden an envelope.

Deciding that her library visit could wait, and wanting some fresh air and exercise, Penny decided to accompany Bronwyn on a walk through the Hawarden Castle parkland before lunch. Bronwyn was especially keen to go as the spot was popular with local dog walkers and, missing her Robbie, she hoped the sight of other dogs would soothe her longing.

Twelve

A few minutes after noon the bishop looked at his watch and decided it was time to wrap up the second session of the morning that had focused on the controversial issue of the ordination of women bishops. While the Church of England had recently voted against it, he saw this as an opportunity for the Church in Wales to demonstrate how in tune it was with contemporary thinking and the wishes of a modern Western society. Minty laughed to herself at the irony of it as she took shorthand notes during the lively discussion. This progressive thinking from the man who treated his own wife with such cold disdain and didn't seem to think her capable of doing very much of anything.

As the session ended, the bishop reminded the group that they were to meet in the dining room for lunch at one, and suggested they could use the time to check their e-mails or read the better daily newspapers so carefully laid out in the Gladstone Room.

As soon as they were out the door, one or two of them thought they might be able to manage a snooze and wasted no time heading upstairs to their rooms.

At one o'clock, the conference delegates reassembled in the dining room queue and eagerly surveyed the lunch offerings: macaroni cheese, chicken korma, and tuna casserole. As at dinner the previous evening, square tables had been pushed together to form one long table so a group of ten could easily sit together. The bishop took his place at one end of the table and his wife at the other, gesturing to the others to sit where they liked. Penny found herself sitting on the right of the bishop's wife, across from Minty Russell. Davies was seated further along, on the same side of the table, on the bishop's left.

Ten minutes later, when everyone had arrived at the table with their lunch choices, the bishop said grace.

"Before we begin eating," said Minty, "I wonder if I might just get a photograph of everyone. We'll want some photos for the parish magazine."

After Minty had taken a few photos up and down the table, Penny took out her phone and snapped photos of the bishop and Davies. The bishop, who feigned a smile, was a fearsome sight.

"Right, well, don't let it get cold," said Pamela Blaine, smiling down the table. "Please, everyone, begin."

"This is the first time we've held this kind of conference," the bishop was saying to Davies. "I think it helps with the teamwork to get everyone together every now and then to discuss issues that affect us all and to share solutions. Make sure we're all singing-from-the-same-hymn-sheet sort of thing. Minty did a brilliant job organizing everything, and we were so pleased that you were able to join us. I found your point about the theft of the copper wiring from the substations most alarming. In fact . . ."

He broke off and looked down the table at the sound of a strange wheezing noise that sounded like a large, desperate intake of breath.

Penny looked across the table and met Minty's eyes. They were opened round and wide and a look of fearful surprise flashed across them. She touched her fingers to her tingling lips and whispered something.

"Epi . . ."

Bronwyn, who was seated beside Davies, turned her head to look down the table and across at Minty.

"Epi . . ." Minty repeated, this time making a clear and emphatic stabbing motion with her finger in the direction of the floor.

"Minty, are you all right? What's the matter?" Bronwyn asked. Minty shook her head.

"Epi . . ." she croaked.

Bronwyn jumped up, pushing back her chair. Her sudden movement startled Davies, who leapt up as well. Bronwyn rushed round the end of the table, behind the startled bishop. "Do you need your EpiPen?" she asked Minty, who nodded vigorously. "Where's your bag?" Minty pointed under her chair. Bronwyn picked it up, opened it, and poked around inside.

"No time for that," said Davies, taking the bag from Bronwyn and dumping its contents on the parquet floor. The two fell to their knees and scrabbled about amongst the items that had tumbled out of the handbag and skittered across the floor. Bronwyn opened a small make-up bag and picked through it, holding up a lipstick and a mascara while Davies opened a wallet, examined pens, riffled the pages of a paperback novel, and turned over various pieces of paper searching frantically for the lifesaving device.

"Call 999 and then tell me what they say," Davies said to Penny as he sat back on his heels. He shook his head and looked at Bronwyn. "There's no EpiPen here." Minty had sunk back in her chair. Her eyes were closed and her face was beginning to swell around the lips and eyes.

"But there's got to be," Bronwyn said. "She always carries one. She told me so herself."

"The ambulance is on its way," Penny said a moment later.

"Are they still on the line? Tell them it's a suspected allergic reaction. Probably food. Tell them she's going into anaphylactic shock. Ask them to hurry."

"Allergic reaction? But how can that be?" Bronwyn asked. "That's not possible. She told me she was allergic to shellfish. Seafood." She gestured at the barely touched plate of chicken korma and rice. "There's no seafood in that. Minty would never have chosen a seafood option and if there had been any seafood, she wouldn't have touched it."

Davies stood up. "Now if everyone would please stay in their seats," he said to the silent, stunned dining room. "Except you, Thomas," he said to Reverend Evans. "I need you to go outside and wait for the paramedics and when they arrive, show them in here. Quick as you like. Stop off at the reception desk and tell them what's happening." As Thomas hurried from the room Davies directed his next remark to the others at the table. "Stay in your seats, please. Nobody move. The paramedics will be here in a moment and we want to give them room to work."

Minty's struggle to breathe became more desperate. She placed a hand over her chest as she gasped for breath and her wheezing grew louder and deeper. Small angry red lesions were starting to appear on her skin.

As the minutes ticked by and the silent tension broken only by Minty's laboured breathing became unbearable, Thomas Evans rushed into the room, pointing to the bishop's table, followed by paramedics pushing a stretcher with several large cases on it.

They bent over Minty and fitted an oxygen mask over her face, then took her vital signs. One of them reached for his case, opened it, removed a syringe, and injected her with its contents. Her eyelids fluttered open, then closed again. She moaned softly. The paramedics worked on her for a few more minutes, then gently lifted her onto the stretcher and covered her with a light blanket.

As she was about to be wheeled out of the dining room, the bishop rose and everyone else in the room followed his lead. "I think a silent prayer is in order," he said when the paramedics had left. All heads bowed obediently. Penny raised her eyes and looked around the table. Bronwyn's honest, decent face was deeply etched with fear and concern.

Hywel Stephens, the accountant, who had arrived sometime that morning and joined the other members of the party at the table for lunch, looked worried, and Shipton had a disengaged look that gave off a vague hint of bored unconcern. Mrs. Blaine, one hand over her mouth, looked curiously angry.

"If anyone feels they'd like to finish their lunch, please do," said the bishop. Shipton immediately raised his knife and fork and began slicing his chicken. Mrs. Blaine pushed her plate away, and the bishop nodded at a hovering member of the kitchen staff to remove it.

When she reached out to take Minty's plate, Davies raised his hand. "Leave it, please," he said. "And don't touch it. But please bring some cling film from the kitchen before you do anything else."

At that moment a loud noise erupted from the direction of the kitchen and the chef, dressed in a professional white jacket, burst into the dining room. His white hair was standing on end and he looked around wildly and then made his way to the clergy table. "What's happened?" he asked. "I heard that someone was taken ill after eating our food. That can't be. Nothing like that has ever happened here. We are very careful with our food handling. Our ingredients are fresh and cooked to highest standard. All our suppliers are local and we observe all the rules. Everything is prepared on site with great care. I don't see how this could have happened."

Davies tried to calm him.

"Sir, we don't know what's happened yet, but someone with a food allergy may have eaten the wrong thing. Nobody is blaming you or accusing you of improper food handling. Now if you wouldn't mind, please, just go back to the kitchen." He gently turned the agitated chef around and watched him return to the kitchen.

Davies then addressed everyone in the room. "Something very serious has happened here and until we know exactly what, we're treating this situation as suspicious. I have to ask that no one leaves the Library unless and until I give permission."

"We had a full program planned for this afternoon," the bishop said. "Break-out groups, financial discussions, that sort of thing. Would it be all right if we carried on?"

Davies nodded. "Indeed, I think that might be for the best, but remember, no one is to leave the building."

"Very well." said the bishop. "But now that we've lost poor Minty, I wonder if we have anyone who could take minutes for us?" He looked hopefully at Stephens, the accountant, who shook his head. "No use asking me and anyway, I'm giving a presentation, remember. I can't do both, can I?"

"Right," said the bishop, looking around with false heartiness. "Well, we'll just have to manage the best we can."

Thomas exchanged a quick glance with Bronwyn. "I could try," he volunteered, "as long as you don't expect too much and don't talk too fast."

"That's the spirit."

The bishop turned to Davies. "You'll keep me informed, won't you?" Davies nodded. The bishop then turned back to the accountant and with his hand on his chin, studied him. "On second thought, Mr. Stephens, I think in light of what's happened here, this afternoon may not be the best time to discuss the financial situation. Absorbing all the information in your presentation will require careful concentration and I don't think we're really up to it." He turned to look at others along the table. "I think we will use the afternoon for reading and quiet contemplation. That's what this Library is for. And if you would be so kind as to speak to us tomorrow, Mr. Stephens, that would be much appreciated.

You'll have to stop over I expect as the police don't want anyone to leave."

"Oh," said Stephens. "I'll need to speak to my wife, of course, in case she has something planned, but it should be all right with her if I stay. I'm away from home a fair bit on business anyway, so she's quite used to it."

"Right. Well, just let them know at reception and I'm sure they'll sort you out." The bishop turned to go.

"Before you go, Bishop, just one more thing," said Davies. "About Miss Russell. Is there someone we can notify? Do you know who her next of kin would be? I gather she's not married, unless of course she prefers to use her maiden name."

"You are correct. She's not married, or at least not to my knowledge. She does have a married sister who lives nearby, I think. She went to visit her recently, just before the conference, in fact. But I'm afraid I don't know anything about her or how you would get in touch. You'd . . ." He gave a helpless shrug. "I almost said you'd have to ask Miss Russell. She looks after all our records—we depend on her totally, my wife and I, to keep us organized."

"Right, well, thank you. Perhaps your wife will know how we can get in touch with the sister. You mentioned she's married. You don't happen to know her married name, do you?"

The bishop shook his head and with a small, tight apology took several steps toward the door. He then stopped and looked back at Davies. "Oh wait. I think I've just remembered something. I seem to recall she mentioned that her brother-in-law works in a pub somewhere around here, if that helps."

A moment later the team of clerics shuffled out of the dining room leaving Penny, Bronwyn, Davies, and Pamela Blaine scattered along the length of the table. Without touching the contents, Davies covered Minty Russell's lunch plate with the cling film the server had delivered while the bishop was speaking. He then reached into his pocket for his phone, stood up, walked to the window, and looking out over the garden while he shuffled back and forth, placed a call. He returned to the table and pulled out the empty chair beside Penny.

"Bethan's on her way to collect the secretary's lunch plate and get it to the lab. We'll have to sit here and keep an eye on it until she arrives to ensure the chain of custody."

"Chain of custody?" asked Bronwyn.

"We have to ensure that the plate we send for forensic testing is this plate," he said, gesturing at it. "The same one Miss Russell ate from. We can't leave it unattended or out of sight so someone has the opportunity to switch it for another."

"But why would someone want to do that?"

"If this plate was tampered with, if someone deliberately added something knowing it could harm Miss Russell, then we want to be able to test for it. And we have to know with one hundred percent certainty that this is the plate that Miss Russell ate from. There can be no doubt about it."

"Do you really think someone deliberately tried to harm her?" asked the bishop's wife.

"I don't know," admitted Davies. "But the fact that there was no EpiPen in her handbag is troubling."

Penny got up from the table and knelt in front of the small pile of contents from Minty's handbag, which were still strewn about the floor. She picked up the shabby leather bag and, one by one, began replacing the contents.

"You did check the side pockets?" she said, looking up at Davies. "Women often keep really important things in the side pockets so they can get at them easily."

"I checked the side pockets, Penny," said Bronwyn. "There was a little book, but I didn't see an EpiPen. Oh dear, I do hope I didn't miss it." She held her hand over her mouth and her eyes were dark with dread.

Penny reached into the last of the side pockets and pulled out a small notebook. She flipped it open and then looked at Davies. "I can't read it."

Page after page was filled with a cacophony of squiggles, lines of varying thickness, circles, loops, and dashes. She held the book up and turned it around so the people at the table could see it.

"Oh," said Bronwyn, "I think I know what that is. It looks like shorthand. Pitman shorthand, I think it's called. I had an aunt who was a secretary and she knew how to do that. Instead of writing the words, you have all those symbols that represent the way words sound. I could never make any sense of it and thought it was wonderful how some people, mainly young women, learned how to do that. It's like a code. They used to teach it at the old secretarial schools." She thought for a moment. "I wonder if secretarial schools still exist. I don't think many girls these days set out to become secretaries and yet it doesn't seem so long ago that secretary was one of the few career options open to women. We've come a long way."

"But you can't read it?" Davies asked.

Bronwyn shook her head. "No, sorry."

He directed a silent enquiry at Mrs. Blaine, who rose stiffly to her feet.

"Of course I can't read it. What do you take me for? And now, if you'll excuse me, I'm finding all this very upsetting. I'd like to go to my room."

"Certainly. But before you go, do you happen to know how we could get in touch with Miss Russell's sister?"

"No, sorry. I have no idea." Davies stood as Pamela Blaine left the dining room, her trim figure attractively displayed from the back in a tight black pencil skirt paired with a well-cut white blouse tapered at the waist. She walked quickly, like a woman who was late for a meeting, her black high heels clicking on the parquet floor.

Davies sat down again and turned to Penny and Bronwyn. "Well, we do have someone we've used in the past who knows shorthand, so I'll ask Bethan to contact her and see if she's available."

"Why do you want to do that?" Bronwyn asked. "Is the notebook important, do you think?"

"It might be, depending on how the investigation goes. We don't know what we're dealing with but we have to consider all possibilities. Hopefully, we'll know more once the contents of the plate have been analyzed."

He checked the time on his phone.

"Bethan'll be here soon to pick it up." He looked from one to the other. "I can't get past the fact that there was no EpiPen in her bag. People with severe allergies always carry one. Always. They never know when they might need it and they know that their lives could depend on it."

He cleared his throat.

"I'd like the two of you to do something for me. Please

keep an eye on the plate while I search Miss Russell's room for the EpiPen. I need to know if the pen was in her room."

Thirty long minutes later a welcome, familiar figure appeared in the dining room entranceway. Catching sight of Penny and Bronwyn at the table, Sgt. Bethan Morgan threaded her way through the tables and joined them. She gave them each a quick greeting and then sat down.

"Where is he?"

"He went to search Miss Russell's room. He wants to know why she didn't have the EpiPen in her bag, so he's looking to see if she left it in her room for some reason. In another bag, maybe," said Bronwyn. "I expect when she's recovered that'll be one of the first things he asks her."

A look of dismay shading into fear flashed across Bethan's face.

"How is she?" Penny asked. "Is she . . . ?"

"She's alive," said Bethan, "but poorly. Her body is shutting down and it doesn't look good."

"She thought the pen was in her bag," said Penny. "As soon as she realized what had happened she pointed at her handbag. She kept trying to tell us to get the EpiPen from her handbag."

At that moment Davies entered the room and as he got closer to the little group he shook his head slightly. Bethan filled him in on Minty's condition and then pulled an evidence bag from her jacket. Davies initialed it and Bethan slid the plate into it, keeping it flat. A few minutes later she was on her way.

"So what happens next?" asked Bronwyn.

"We wait and see," said Davies, picking up the notebook and examining the coded contents.

They did not have long to wait. A few minutes later Davies's phone rang. He listened for a moment, then nodded.

"Yes, I'm sure you did. Yes, there'll have to be one." He listened for a few more moments, thanked the caller, and then rang off. The little group raised fearful eyes in his direction.

"Miss Russell died ten minutes ago. There'll have to be a postmortem. No question about that."

Thirteen

In the downstairs hall of Evelyn Lloyd's comfortable house on Rosemary Lane in Llanelen, Florence Semble put the phone down and turned around just in time to see Mrs. Lloyd dart back into the sitting room. A moment later, her head emerged and the rest of her sidled through the doorway.

"Well?" asked Mrs. Lloyd eagerly. "I was deeply engrossed in *The Lady*, but you were talking so loudly I couldn't help overhear a bit of your conversation. It certainly sounded intriguing."

"That was the North Wales Police. They have a job for me and I'm to come at once. I'm to plan to stay overnight."

"A job for you? What kind of job could you possibly do for the North Wales Police? What on earth are you talking about?"

Florence rested her hand on the banister, one foot on the first stair.

"A woman's died in what they call suspicious circumstances. She left a notebook, but it's written in shorthand. They need me to translate it for them. And," she added proudly, "although I would be happy to do it as the good civic-minded citizen I am, they're going to pay me. It's considered translation. A professional service."

Mrs. Lloyd folded her hands in front of her. In a recent television documentary she had seen the Queen working in her office, wearing a simple, tailored dress with a brooch on the left shoulder and black shoes with low heels. Thinking the outfit exactly what a lady should wear at home in the daytime, Mrs. Lloyd had adopted the same look. Her dress was a burgundy wool and her brooch was an ornate, swirling flower made up of pink and red stones.

"Now when they said come at once, Florence, do they mean to send a car for you?"

"No. I'm to take the train to Chester, letting them know which train I'm on, and they'll send a car to the station to meet me."

"Us," said Mrs. Lloyd firmly. "They'll send a car to meet us."

She consulted her wristwatch. "I think there's a train in about two hours, but I'll check the schedule and ring for the taxi while you get ready." She thought for a moment. "We'll need to take some sandwiches with us for the journey. We don't want to waste our money on that awful rubbish you get on the train. There's that leftover roast beef. That would be good. What do you think?" Without waiting for an answer, she went on. "Oh, and we'll definitely need a flask of tea. It's been ages since I used the flask. I wonder where I put it? I hope it wasn't in with the lot I sent along to Bronwyn for the spring jumble sale. Well, we'll have a look for it. It must be somewhere." She took a step toward the kitchen. "And some wine gums. I always like wine gums on a train journey, for some reason. Have we got any in?"

Florence shook her head. "Why would we have wine gums hanging about?"

"No? Well, we'll just stop off and pick up a couple of packets on the way to the station. And I'll bring a couple of my magazines." She looked at Florence. "I suppose you have your library book?"

Florence remained where she was, one hand still on the banister.

"Well, don't just stand there, Florence. We've got a lot do. You start with the sandwiches and I'll take care of the travel arrangements."

"Evelyn, it's me they want. Not us. Not you. I'm perfectly capable of doing this on my own."

Mrs. Lloyd had the decency to look mildly apologetic.

"Of course you are, Florence. There's no doubt about that or they wouldn't have asked you. But I haven't been any-where for ages, and surely you would not begrudge me ac-companying you, would you?" Eyes bright with enthusiasm, she added, "I could be your assistant."

"Do you know shorthand, Evelyn?"

"No, I could never make head nor tail of it."

Florence laughed. "Then I don't really see how you could be my assistant."

"I will offer unqualified support and encouragement, Florence, as you set about your important police work. Now, where did you say we were going, exactly?" asked Mrs. Lloyd.

"I didn't say, but it's Gladstone's Library. And I think you meant unconditional support, not unqualified."

"Oh, wonderful!" exclaimed Mrs. Lloyd, clapping her hands. "There you are, you see! I've heard so much about Gladstone's Library and always wanted to go there, so this is the perfect opportunity. A day or two away will do me so much good."

Florence frowned.

"Oh, Florence, you didn't really think I'd let you have this adventure all on your own, did you? This is much too good to miss." She thought a moment. "And wait until Penny Brannigan hears about this. That we," knowing when not to push her luck, Mrs. Lloyd corrected herself, "that you were asked to go to a murder to provide assistance to the police. So exciting. Thrilling, even."

"I think she knows already."

"What? How could she possibly . . ."

"It was her boyfriend, that Inspector Davies, who rang me. Penny was the one who suggested I might be able to help sort out the shorthand. Apparently there was someone they used in the past, but it's been so long since they needed her that she's died, so Penny suggested me. She remembered that I used to work as a secretary at the Liverpool College of Art back in the old days and thought I might know shorthand, which I do."

"I might have known," grumbled Mrs. Lloyd. "What is it about that woman, that wherever and whenever there's a murder, there she is."

"And mind your language, Evelyn. Nobody said anything about murder. Suspicious circumstances they called it."

Florence turned toward the kitchen.

"Right, then. I'd best get on with those sandwiches. But you do know, Evelyn, that the train journey doesn't take much over an hour from Llandudno. We're not taking the overnight train to Scotland. And I'm sure there'll be plenty for us to eat when we get there. We're not likely to starve."

Fourteen

How are you going to spend what's left of the afternoon, Penny?" asked Bronwyn. "I don't expect we'll see much of Gareth from now on. We'll have to amuse ourselves." Davies had left them soon after Bethan had set off to deliver the contents of Minty Russell's luncheon plate to the forensics lab. He wanted to interview the kitchen staff himself. With the right handling, the chef might be able to help with the inquiry.

"I thought I'd do some sketching in the garden," Penny replied, "while the light is still good. Gardens are beautiful to me all year round. Care to join me? I'd welcome the company."

"Would you? I wasn't sure."

"I'm not too keen on people looking over my shoulder while I work, but I like having people nearby, if you know what I mean. That's why our little sketching group works so well. There's always someone close, but not too close."

A few years earlier, Penny and a few like-minded friends had formed the Stretch and Sketch Club for amateur drawing and painting enthusiasts, and the occasional photographer, who enjoyed rambling about the countryside, capturing the beautiful, varied scenery in all its Welsh greenery and glory.

"That wasn't exactly what I meant about wondering if you wanted company, but if you're sure, I'll get my book and I might just bring a cup of coffee with me. I'll see you outside in a few minutes."

"I'll be round the back. Where the statues are." Penny clutched her satchel of art supplies under one arm, and warmly dressed against the light, but cool, breeze, she slipped out the door near the chapel, to the sculpture garden where Bronwyn found her a few minutes later.

Bronwyn sat at one of the picnic tables beside Penny, set her book down and took a sip of coffee. She watched Penny sketch for a few minutes. "Penny, about what I said earlier. It's just that I was wondering if you were coming out here because you wanted some time on your own. If you don't mind my asking, is everything all right between you and Gareth? Only you don't seem as, oh, I don't know, comfortable with him as you used to. You used to have a bit of sparkle when you were around him and that seems to be gone. You seem anxious around him."

Penny looked up from her sketching pad.

"It's that obvious, is it?"

"Maybe just to me. Do you want to talk about it?"

Penny put down her pencil.

"I've been thinking a lot about this the past few days. I would say that my feelings toward him haven't changed. In fact, quite the opposite. But part of me is pulling back, trying to disengage, not letting myself go there." She sighed. "Victoria has suggested that he's going to ask me to marry him and I rather hope he won't. I don't want that kind of major change in my life. I like things the way they are." After a moment she added, "The way we are." She gave a helpless shrug. "But I don't want to hurt him, and I certainly don't want to lose our friendship, so I'm not sure how to handle the situation. I don't know how to tell him how I really feel without it sounding like a rejection."

"Well, then, Penny, if you're sure this is how you feel and you don't just need more time, you must raise the subject, tactfully, of course, before he does, so he knows not to ask you. That way, he'll be spared the embarrassment of a rejection."

Penny groaned. "That sounds like the sensible thing to do."

"I had a magazine from the library recently on how to phrase difficult things in ways that are not harsh or hurtful. Would you like me to help with the words? Apparently you should speak from the heart in a sincere manner and start with something positive and encouraging."

"You mean like, 'It's not you, it's me.'?"

Bronwyn laughed. "Oh, I think you can do better than that. But do think about saying something to him, so he knows." A small silence fell over them, broken only by the wispy sound of Penny's pencil on her sketch pad. And then Bronwyn spoke.

"Part of what you're feeling, Penny, may be related to

what you've got used to. You've been on your own for a very long time, so the idea of having a deep, all-consuming, committed relationship with someone may seem just too much for you. It works the other way, too, of course. That's why someone who's been married for donkey's years finds it so difficult to adjust to being alone when the spouse dies. I simply cannot imagine my life without Thomas. I would be so lost without him. Bereft. I depend on him for everything. Almost every thought I have is us and we, not I or me. That's the way of people who have been married happily for a long time. Perhaps your problem is you cannot imagine your life defined by being with Gareth, to any great extent. The extent of being married to him. Perhaps you feel you'd have to give up too much of yourself to do that."

"I almost married someone, once," Penny replied.

"I remember," said Bronwyn. "Tim. But that was a long time ago. How old were you when he died?"

"Thirty-three. He died just a few days after my birthday."

"And there's never really been anyone in your life since then, has there? Until Gareth came along, that is. Does Gareth know about Tim, by the way?"

Penny nodded. "I told him, but he might not remember. I told him the very first time we went out."

Bronwyn gave a small indication that she'd heard and then bowed her head over her book as Penny returned to her sketching. Sunlight filtered onto her page as a bird sang lustily in the budding branches that shifted back and forth above them. Penny set her pencil down and covered her mouth while she yawned.

"I don't know, Bronwyn, I might think about having a nap," she said. "It's been a dreadful day. Just awful."

"What do you make of it all, Penny?"

"I haven't a clue. I've been wracking my brain to see if there's anything there that might help." She leaned forward, her hands clasped between her knees. "Have you ever noticed that when something happens and it becomes important to remember all the details, how difficult that can be?"

Bronwyn turned toward her.

"What do you mean?"

Penny thought for a moment as she tried to come up with an example. "Well, let's say, for example, that you lose your house keys while you're walking Robbie." Bronwyn nodded. "So in your mind you retrace every step you took. Where you stopped. What you did. Were the keys in a bag, in your hand, or in your pocket? Did you pull something out of your pocket? Could the keys have come out then and fallen to the ground? If they landed on the pavement you'd hear a clink. If they fell on grass, you might not hear them. Did you have your keys in your hand when you just popped into a shop to pick something up and could you have set your keys down on the counter while you paid? Were you distracted, not paying attention to what you were doing? And so on."

Bronwyn nodded. "Yes, I see all that, but I don't quite see what it has to do with what happened to Minty."

"Well, I'm trying to remember everything that happened at lunch, but I can't remember all the details. Details that could be important. Who did she speak to? Where was everybody? Did anyone leave the table? And her handbag. Where was her handbag? That's the important thing. Did she have it with her at all times? Was it draped over her shoulder or was she carrying it? Or did she, as we all do, set it down somewhere for a few minutes while she, oh, I don't know, went through the queue with her tray and chose what she was having for lunch. Did she go into the dining room first and leave her handbag at the table so her hands would be free to carry the tray? There are so many small details that later turn out to be important, but at the time we didn't know they were important, so we took no notice. But if she'd left her handbag unattended, that could be vital to the investigation. Who had access to it today? Or maybe you can recall what happened at the reception last night. Was her handbag left unattended then?"

"Yes, I see what you mean now. Let me think." Bronwyn leaned back. "I'll try to visualize it." She closed her eyes and held her hands loosely over them, her fingertips just touching her hairline. "We were at the opening reception in the Gladstone Room and she went from person to person. She spoke to the bishop, I definitely remember that. Did she also speak to his wife? I don't remember the wife doing anything much at the reception. There was a problem with Reverend Shipton and his boyfriend. The bishop was very cross that he had brought him. Actually, I'm not sure *cross* is the right word. You could practically see the smoke coming out his ears. Beside himself. Furious. Anyway, I offered to help Minty find the right words to handle the situation, but she went over and spoke to them, Shipton and his boyfriend. What she said to them, I don't know, but the Nigerian man left the conference soon after, I believe, and Reverend Shipton stayed behind on his own. He didn't seem very happy, but honestly, what did he expect? Minty said she'd warned him that his friend would not be welcome and he brought him anyway. So no one to blame but himself, really."

She opened her eyes and touched Penny's arm.

"Wait. There was one thing, though. We were talking about her allergy to shellfish and she mentioned the EpiPen. She said something like, 'I always have it with me,' as she patted her handbag. So she must have had it with her then, and now that I think about it, she believed that it was in her bag today."

"You're right," agreed Penny. "When she realized what was happening to her, she said 'Epi' very clearly and pointed under her chair at her bag, like this." Penny made a little downward stabbing motion. "She thought the pen was in her bag, where she always kept it and where she expected it to be."

"So someone must have removed the pen."

"It looks like that, doesn't it?"

"Come on, let's go find Gareth."

"Oh," said Bronwyn, her eyes bright with enthusiasm. "Do you think we've come up with a clue? How exciting."

"It might be. I've learned that the best thing to do is just tell him everything and let him decide what's important. It drives him crazy when people know something that actually turns out to be important and didn't tell the police because they didn't think it was relevant. But they don't know what else is going on or what the police are looking for so they have no idea what's relevant." She slipped her pencil in her satchel and stood while Bronwyn gathered up her coffee cup and book.

"But I do think this is important," said Penny.

Fifteen

They found Davies in discussion with Warden Graham Fletcher in the Gladstone Room. Both heads turned toward the door and both men rose from the comfortable brown chairs as the women entered.

"Gareth, Bronwyn's remembered something that might be important," Penny said. Davies took a step toward her and then turned to Fletcher.

"Warden, would you excuse us, please?"

"Yes, of course," he said. "I was just leaving, anyway. Lots to attend to. Let me know if you need anything. All the staff are at your disposal. We're happy to help in any way we can. Just let us know what you need. You've only to ask."

"Thank you, Warden," said Davies, as Fletcher closed the door quietly behind him.

"Oh, I'm sorry," said Penny. "I should have realized you'd need to speak to him." Davies shook his head slightly and then turned to Bronwyn. He listened while she recounted her conversation with Minty Russell at the previous night's welcoming drinks party and reception. "So you see, she expected the EpiPen to be in her bag, didn't she? Does that mean that someone took it, do you think?"

"It might," said Davies. "I searched her room and didn't find it."

"What's going to happen next?" asked Penny.

"Well, we're definitely classifying this death as suspicious and we've referred it to the coroner but a postmortem is a foregone conclusion. So we'll await the results of that. And then we'll wait to see if the coroner calls an inquest, as I suspect he will. In the meantime, we'll interview everyone who was at lunch and everyone who worked here. And we'll be looking into Miss Russell's past."

Bronwyn tipped her head to one side with a quizzical expression, as Davies continued.

"Because almost every murder—not the random, psycho kind, but the ordinary, everyday kind—is committed for either love or money. We'll do some digging and see what we can turn up."

The two women exchanged puzzled glances.

"What's the matter?" Davies asked.

"Well, it's just that from what we could tell, Minty didn't seem to have much of either. Love or money. So why would someone want to kill her?" Bronwyn asked.

"*If* someone killed her," Davies reminded her, emphasizing the word if. "And I'm not saying she was murdered.

Although it's certainly beginning to look like it. Someone knew about her allergy and then made sure her EpiPen wasn't there when she needed it."

Bronwyn shuddered.

"I wonder if someone overheard her saying at the opening night party that she had allergies," said Bronwyn.

"That's a possibility," said Davies. "Can you remember who was standing beside you? Near you? Within earshot?"

Bronwyn shook her head. "If I'd known then that it might be important I'd have taken more notice. Penny and I were just discussing that. At the time, it was just a fairly large group of people socializing over a glass of wine."

"Did anyone take photos?" Davies asked.

"I don't think so. I didn't see anyone taking photos," Bronwyn replied.

"Well, we'll see what the investigation turns up."

"What are you going to do now?" asked Penny.

"Ring Bethan to see what time she'll be here with Florence. They should be here soon. In the meantime, what are you two going to do?"

Bronwyn and Penny exchanged glances.

"We thought it was time we visited the Library. The Library proper, that is. We haven't seen it yet. Bronwyn was going to go earlier with Thomas, but they just popped in. Didn't really do it justice."

"Well, let's go, then. I'll walk with you."

As they reached the reception area, the door opened and Bethan entered, carrying a small overnight bag and a large suitcase. She was followed by Florence, who looked around her appreciatively. And a moment later Bronwyn gave a small gasp as Mrs. Lloyd entered the reception area.

"Hello!" she said gaily to the little group. "It's not quite *Downton Abbey,* is it? But it'll do very well for the likes of us."

Sixteen

"I've made arrangements for you to work in the Gladstone Room, Florence," said Davies, leading her down the corridor. "The light is very good in there."

"Oh, my, isn't this interesting?" Florence smiled, pausing to look at the photographs and Gladstone memorabilia displayed in cases lining the corridor. She stopped in front of the case nearest the wooden door that led to the Gladstone Room and pointed. "Look at that!" She peered at the glass. "Plates and a jug with Gladstone's image on them. I thought all that was a modern marketing gimmick designed to sell loads of tat at royal weddings and of course, the Jubilee. Biscuit tins, teapots, tea towels, and such. But look, it's been going on since," she leaned closer, "well, the late 1800s, anyway, if not before." She thought for a moment. "You know, when I was young I had an elderly aunt who had so many framed photographs of Winston Churchill all over the place, I grew up thinking he was a relative of ours."

Davies gave a light laugh. "There's even more Gladstone stuff inside," he said, opening the door for her.

She entered the large, beautifully proportioned room slowly, taking in the carefully arranged brown leather sofas and chairs, burgundy carpet, and soft lighting. "It reminds me a little of the old senior common room at the Art College, but much nicer," observed Florence. "It's how you would picture an old-fashioned gentlemen's club. Not that I've ever set foot in such a place, being a woman, but you used to see them in the pictures, sometimes." She pointed to a sturdy oak table on which fresh, folded copies of the better daily newspapers were artfully arranged. "Or maybe it's just what I would imagine a gentlemen's club to be."

"I think you may be right," said Davies. "Now, would you like to work at this table? It's big enough so you can spread out."

Florence looked at him anxiously. "I hope I can provide the level of service you require, Inspector. I know this is important work and my translation must be accurate. I think my skills are still sharp enough, but unfortunately I no longer have my dictionary. I got rid of it when I moved from Liverpool. You can't keep everything, can you? I seem to get rid of things and later, wish I'd kept them. And then I look at something I've had for years and think, 'Why am I hanging on to that old thing?'"

"Well, don't worry about the dictionary, Florence. I've checked and although this library doesn't run to one, there's a public library almost next door and they might have one.

And if they don't, we'll find a way. There might be such a thing online and if so, we can bring in a laptop for you."

"Oh, I don't know about that," Florence replied. "I don't have much experience with computers. I retired before they really came in, you see, and I just never felt the need to learn how to use one."

"Of course. Well, as I said, don't worry about it. If you do need to use a computer we'll make sure someone is here to help you."

Davies pulled out a chair. As Florence smiled at him he realized how much that small gesture meant. She was much more used to being the one who did the assisting rather that the one being helped.

Davies sat at a right angle to her rather than across the table.

"The warden has placed a Reserved sign on the door to let people know the room is in use. You won't be disturbed." He reached into a large bag and pulled out a new, lined notebook, two pens and finally, Minty Russell's steno book. At the sight of it, Florence leaned forward. "Haven't seen one of those for a while," she remarked as Davies handed it to her.

"I want you to transcribe everything that's in here. Don't try to work out if something is important or not. Let me decide that." He gestured at the notebook. "It's up to you if you want to write it out or if you want me to get you a laptop so you can type, but from what you just told me I'm guessing you'd want to write it in the notebook. But if you prefer, I could get a police officer here to type as you dictate."

"Let's start with the notebook and see how I go," said Florence. Davies pushed his chair back and stood up. "Right, well, I'll be on my way. I'm glad you agreed to do this for us and were able to spare the time."

"I'm glad I can help," Florence said. "Or try to, any road. But there is something else I wanted to say before you go, Inspector. I'm very sorry about Evelyn coming along. I did try to explain that this was business and she wasn't really wanted but it seemed hard to do that without being unkind." She gave a helpless little shrugging gesture. "You know what she's like. She was that determined to come. Making plans and giving orders, she was, before I'd barely had a chance to put the phone down."

"Indeed, I do know what she's like," smiled Davies. "But don't give her another thought. Bronwyn and Penny have agreed to keep her entertained and out of trouble, so you're all right."

He checked his watch. "I've asked for . . ." He was interrupted by the sound of knocking on the door. Davies opened it, reached out to take something, and then returned to Florence at the table.

Setting down a nicely laid out tea tray, he gave her a reassuring smile.

"I'll check back in an hour or so to see how you're getting on, but if you need anything in the meantime, just ask at reception and they'll find me. But if you do leave the room, make sure you take everything with you. Don't leave even a scrap of paper behind." He nudged the tray across the table a little closer to her. "Do you need anything else or shall I leave you to get on with it?"

"I think I've got everything I need, thanks."

"Right, then." Davies closed the door quietly behind him. Florence admired the attractive tea tray that had been set before her; she couldn't remember the last time someone had brought her a tea tray, but over the years she'd delivered plenty of them to other people. It was nice to be waited on, for a change. She picked up the teapot, poured a cup, added a spoonful of sugar, and gave it a slow stir. The shortbread biscuits looked homemade and her first nibble confirmed they were. She took a sip of tea, wiped her hands on the snowy white napkin, and reveled in an unfamiliar sense of luxurious well-being. What it must be like to live like this, she thought. To be able to read and work in calm, comfortable surroundings with nothing to worry about and your every need met.

After taking one last appreciative look around the room, she opened Minty Russell's steno pad and set to work.

Seventeen

*T*wo hours later Florence put down her pen, took off her glasses, rubbed her eyes, and glanced at the window. Dusk was closing in. So far, she'd seen nothing out of the ordinary in Minty's notebook. There were straightforward minutes from various meetings and notes for one or two letters that the bishop had asked her to draft. But all that was more or less what she'd expected to find. She stood up and strolled over to the fireplace, then walked to a large bookcase filled with contemporary novels. She scanned the titles on the spines, ran her fingers over one or two, and pulled one off the shelf. After reading the jacket notes and discovering the story took place in North Wales, she carried it with her back to the table and checked her watch. The inspector had said he'd be back in an hour, and now almost two hours had gone by so he should be along soon.

A few minutes later the door opened and there he was. He joined her at the table.

"Now, then, Florence, how'd you get on?"

"All right, I think. There are minutes from meetings and notes for correspondence, all rather routine and ordinary. It's all in here." She pushed the notebook toward him. "All recent. There wasn't that much. The steno book was quite new. I found the notes from your presentation on church thefts very interesting."

The corners of his mouth drooped slightly. He took off his glasses and rubbed his eyes.

"Don't be disappointed, Inspector. What's in here is exactly what you'd expect to find. I could tell from the quality of her work that she had been well trained. She was very professional."

"You could tell all that, could you, just from her notebook?"

"Oh, yes, Inspector." Florence gestured at the notebook. "You see, we were taught that these notebooks belong to our employer and that they are the next best thing to a legal document. There should not be anything untoward or personal in this book." She patted the neatly written transcribed pages she had just completed. "You'll want to go over everything, I'm sure, in case there's something there that means something to you, but I saw nothing unusual in the minutes of the meetings or drafts of letters. All very routine, in my opinion."

Davies nodded.

"But there is something."

Davies eyes widened slightly and his gaze became more intense. Florence opened the stenographer's notebook. It was spiral bound along the top and when opened fully, lay flat on the table. "As I said, her steno book contained only work-related notes, but it may be that she did use the notebook to record personal information." Florence pointed to a small shred of paper caught in the coiled binding. "You can see here where a page has been ripped out of the notebook, leaving this little bit of paper behind. The page that's been torn out could very well have been personal. As a properly trained stenographer, she would not have left personal notes in her official notebook." Florence shook her head slightly. "Now, I am not saying the page contained anything important." She gave a slight shrug and raised her hands in a small gesture. "I don't know what it contained. It could be no more than a shopping list or a list of things she needed to do that she wrote in the middle of a boring meeting. I used to do that sort of thing myself. Or, it could be something important." She flipped several pages. "And see, another page has been torn out here. In fact, this was the second last entry in the book, just before the notes she took of your talk on the church thefts, so it's very recent. It might be of some significance. I don't know." Florence gave Davies an encouraging look. "So if I were you, Inspector, I'd look a little harder and see if these missing pages turn up. And if you find them, they might also be in shorthand and if they are, I'd be happy to translate them for you."

"Thank you, Florence. I appreciate your work today." Davies placed the steno notebook in an evidence bag and gathered up the rest of the materials. "I'm going to ask you to stand by. Her office is being searched now and if anything turns up, I'll let you know." They stood up. "Now, I'm sure you're ready for another cup of tea."

"Something a little stronger, I think, Inspector, if you wouldn't mind," replied Florence, tipping her head in the direction of the honesty bar which resembled a tempting, well-stocked drinks table in the drawing room of a country house. Miniatures of liquor were set out, along with small cans of mixers, a variety of glasses, bottles of wine and sherry, a filled ice bucket, and a small plate of sliced lemon, covered in cling film.

"Good idea," said Davies, "I wish I could join you but I've still got a lot of work to do today. What can I get you? Sherry, is it?"

"Do you know, Inspector, I'd like something a little different. Let's push the boat out. Mine's a gin and tonic with ice, please."

"Mrs. Lloyd has been asking when you're likely to be finished. Shall I send her in or would you like to enjoy your drink on your own?" Davis asked as he snapped open a can of tonic water.

"Has Penny been looking after her?"

"She has."

"Poor Penny. Better send Evelyn in, then."

Davies laughed as he added a slice of lemon to her drink.

"That's very understanding of you, Florence. Would Mrs. Lloyd like a drink, too, do you think?"

"Yes, Inspector, I'm sure she would. Would you mind making it two?"

"Not at all. Does she take ice with hers, too?" Davies signed for both drinks and then reached for the tongs.

Eighteen

*D*avies found Penny and Mrs. Lloyd seated in the dining room, looking out over the back garden. A moment after hearing that Florence had a drink waiting for her in the Gladstone Room, Mrs. Lloyd scuttled away, leaving Penny and Davies with the room to themselves. The metal shutter of the servery window was closed as the kitchen staff finished preparations for the evening meal. The dining room was empty and silent, except for the occasional sound of Alan, the chef, calling out an order to the kitchen staff over the rattle of large pots and pans.

"Any new developments?" Penny asked. "Was Florence able to help at all?"

"Possibly. She didn't see anything of interest in the steno book, but she did make an interesting observation. It's not what's there that could be important, but what isn't there."

"Meaning?"

"Meaning that at least two pages that could contain personal information seem to be missing. I've asked for Minty's office to be searched. If the pages turn up, in her desk, say, they may be important or, as Florence said, they may contain nothing more than a shopping list. Anyway, if and when we find them, Florence will translate for us if need be."

"What do you make of all this?" Penny asked. "This whole business with Minty."

"It seems likely that someone deliberately put shellfish on her plate, knowing that she had a severe allergy to it. Whether that person wanted to frighten her or kill her, I don't know. But the PM is scheduled for first thing in the morning so hopefully we'll get some useful information from that, although the toxicology results will take longer."

Penny nodded. "It would be helpful to know who was within earshot at the reception when she mentioned her allergy. Bronwyn said she was speaking in a normal voice so anyone nearby could have heard her."

"But we don't know enough about her yet to know why someone would want to hurt her," said Davies.

The two lapsed into a silence that, as the seconds turned into a minute, hung heavy and awkward. Where once there had been companionable silence, now there was awkwardness with a hint of underlying tension.

"This isn't turning out the way I'd hoped it would," Davies said finally.

"No," Penny replied. "It's too bad about Minty."

"I think you know I didn't mean that, Penny, although that situation is certainly not helping. I meant between you and me. I'd hoped that this time away together would have been enjoyable for you. Spending time together. Just the two of us. I'd hoped that we . . ."

He looked at her, beseechingly, but she did not meet his eyes. "What is it, Penny? What's the matter?" When she did not reply, he continued, softly. "Look, I'm not stupid. I read people's body language for a living. I know there's something wrong and I'm hoping we can talk about it. That you feel comfortable enough to tell me what it is. Or what you're feeling. You can be honest with me, you know."

Finally, she raised her troubled eyes to meet his anxious ones, then looked away.

"I don't know," she said, softly. "But I do know it isn't you or anything you've done." She covered her eyes with her fingers and shook her head lightly. "Oh, this is going to sound stupid, I know. It's just that this has got too intense and it scares me a bit." She peered at him and smiled. "And at the same time I value our friendship so highly and I'm afraid of losing that." She shrugged and locking her fingers together, placed her hands on the table, and looked at them. "I don't want things to change. I liked how comfortable we were before things got complicated."

"But did things get complicated?" he asked gently. "Or are we just moving on to the logical place where good relationships go?" He covered her hand with his and was relieved when she did not pull hers away. "Penny, tell me. What are you afraid of? What's this really about?"

But before she could answer, his phone rang. He glanced at the caller ID and then, with an apologetic grimace, answered it, listened for a few minutes, and then rang off.

"That was the pathologist's office. The PM's been moved up—it's going to take place this evening, so I have to go.

Sorry, love. We'll continue this conversation, but all I want is for you to be happy, and I'm fine with whatever you want. We'll take things as they come and as slowly as you like. No pressure." He leaned over, put his hand on her shoulder and kissed her cheek. "Really. No pressure." As he got to his feet she looked up at him and smiled and a moment later he was gone. She remained where she was, enjoying the feelings of relief washing over her that the conversation they needed to have had been started. Then, she too left the room.

As she reached the top of the stairs and turned down the hall toward the bedrooms, she heard low, urgent voices coming from the Robinson Room. She walked just past the open door and flattened herself against the wall.

"I told you, darling, we'd have to be careful," a male voice said. Penny gave a tiny gasp at hearing almost the very same words that had been left on her voice mail and covered her mouth with her hand. After a moment, a female voice responded, "Well, we certainly weren't expecting anything like this. I think we'd better finish, don't you? It's all just become too risky and if I'm honest, just a little bit boring. Anyway, it's been fun, but we've gone as far as we can, wouldn't you agree? There doesn't seem much point anymore."

When there was no reply, the female voice went on, "You didn't have anything to do with it, did you? With what happened to the precious Miss Russell?" The male voice gave a little noise of what sounded like disgust and as the door started to open Penny took five fast steps down the hall and turned around so she appeared to be coming toward the Robinson Room. A moment later, Hywel Stephens emerged, followed by Pamela Blaine.

Penny gave them a weak smile and said hello, but they

ignored her. Head down, Mrs. Blaine brushed past her, and the accountant headed in the opposite direction, through the door that led to the landing at the top of the stairs. A few moments later his feet made soft thudding sounds on the carpeted stairs.

Nineteen

Elwy Nash paused to collect his thoughts on the doorstep of the small bungalow just outside Hawarden where he lived with his wife, Constance. He had terrible news for her, and needed to take a moment to find the right words.

He put the key in the lock and let himself in. He hung his jacket on a hook in the hall and pushed open the door to the sitting room. His wife, her head covered in a scarf patterned with yellow roses, dozed in a heavy brown recliner, her feet elevated on the raised footrest. Her head lolled against the back of the chair, her mouth slightly open. The soft hiss of a gas fire and a ticking clock on the mantelpiece broke the silence in the stifling, overheated room.

He sat down on the sofa and gazed at her until she stirred and turned her head toward him.

"So. You're home, then," she said.

"Yes, Constance, I'm home and I've got some very bad news. It's about Minty, I'm afraid. The police came to see me in the pub this afternoon."

His wife struggled to sit up.

"Don't get up, pet. Just listen to what I've got to say and brace yourself. Something terrible happened at the Library today around lunchtime. We saw the ambulance arrive and a punter came in a bit later and said someone had been taken away with a bad case of food poisoning."

Constance closed her eyes and her lashes started to glisten.

"I'm sorry, love. I guess I'd better just come out and say it." He leaned forward and took his wife's hand. "It's Minty. She ate some kind of shellfish apparently and had a bad reaction. Very bad. They took her to the hospital and they did everything they could for her, but she died." He paused for a moment to let it sink in. "They said she wouldn't have suffered. I'm really sorry, pet. I couldn't think of any way to tell you that would make it easier for you."

Constance opened her eyes. "My sister? Minty? But how can that be? She was always so careful. There must be some mistake."

"The police said it was her, love. They asked if I would identify the body and I did. That's why I'm late getting back. It's her, all right."

His wife glared at him. "Lunchtime, was it? I'll never believe this was an accident. She was always so careful. She knew how serious that allergy was and she always carried that pen thing, that device that you inject yourself with, in case she should eat some seafood by mistake." She glared at him. "What did the police say? What do they think happened?"

"They said they're investigating."

"'Well, they'd better be." She thought for a moment and then her eyes widened slightly. "You two always hated each other, you and Minty, and you know what Mother thought of you. That's why she left everything to Minty, so you couldn't get your hands on it. Did you have anything to do with this?"

Elwy looked shocked. "Of course I didn't."

"But you knew she'd be at that conference. You knew about her terrible allergy to shellfish. It would have been easy for you to slip over to the Library on your lunch hour and tamper with her food."

"How would I do that?"

"It would have been easy. You could have borrowed a white coat from the kitchen at the pub, walked to the Library, entered through the kitchen entrance, and while everyone was busy with lunch service, they'd have taken no notice of you. I saw that in a movie, once. And then you hide something deadly on Minty's plate and slip out before anyone even knows you've been there."

"What a load of old rubbish! How could you even think such a thing?"

His wife's eyes hardened and glittered. "I'm not going to sit here and listen to this," he said, getting up. "Look, I'm sorry your sister's dead. You're right, she and I never did get on, but kill her? Never. Why would I?"

"Because now everything belongs to me. Everything that Mother left and now Minty's estate as well, what there is of it. Even Granny's pearls. Well, you needn't think you'll ever see one penny of any of it. So if you did kill her, you've just gone and done it for nothing. Nothing!"

The sitting room door slammed behind him. Exhausted, Constance leaned back in her chair and began to weep.

A few minutes later the door opened and Elwy crept in carrying a cup of tea. "I have to say I'm really hurt that you could even think such a thing, Constance. It's true that Minty and I didn't get on and we've fallen out over the years. But you've had a terrible shock and you're not yourself. I know that. You're just lashing out because you're upset."

He took a few steps into the room and set the cup on a small table beside her chair. "Thought you might need that. I put lots of sugar in it. For the shock, like. I came back to tell you the police said the postmortem would be tonight and they'll release the body as soon as they can." He waited for a response and when there was none, he asked, "Do you want me to leave you alone now?"

Constance shook her head so he eased himself slowly onto the sofa to be near her. His wife's frail body convulsed as racking sobs overwhelmed it. He reached out for her hand and his heart almost broke as he picked it up. The hand that used to hoist luggage, roll out pastry, and hang out wet laundry on a summer morning now felt like a soft bag filled with bird bones. She clasped his as tightly as she could.

Penny opened the door to the Library chamber. Although she had thought the Library would look its best in the full light of day, she was mistaken. Bathed in the soft glow of table lamps that tempered the harsher illumination of overhead fluorescent lighting, the Library at dusk was a magical sight. With its warm oak fittings, rows and rows of multicoloured books, leaded windows, statuary, hidden alcoves and recesses, and brown leather straight-back Parsons chairs it was an awe-inspiring, yet practical, place. The upstairs level, where deep shadows gathered in the corners, was dark, mysterious, and slightly forbidden. She stood in the doorway, taking it all in, then let the door close gently behind her, thinking that by candlelight, which would never be allowed, this chamber would be enchanting.

Twenty

*P*amela Blaine must have given up on the conference," Bronwyn remarked to Penny as the two sat finishing their coffee. Breakfast service had ended and they were the last ones left in the dining room. "She wasn't down for breakfast and I haven't seen her since, oh, since Minty was taken ill at that awful lunch, I guess. And that seems like ages ago."

When Penny did not reply, Bronwyn added, "She may even have gone home, for all I know."

"I saw her yesterday coming out of the Robinson Room," Penny said. "But I didn't speak to her."

"Well, to change the subject," Bronwyn said, "What do you think we should do this morning? Or are you going to stay on for a bit? I suppose you could go home any time you like, really."

"I could," agreed Penny. "And I should be getting back to the Spa. Mrs. Lloyd and Florence and I talked it over and we're taking the train home together this afternoon. So this morning I thought I might walk through the parkland as far as Hawarden Castle. You can't get too close to it as the Gladstone family still lives there, apparently, and it's all private land, but I would like to get out and walk a bit further. I'll take some materials with me and if there's anything worth sketching, I'll spend some time doing that."

Bronwyn nodded. "Well, I have my book, so I think I'll stay inside and read. In the Library, I think. Seems funny to bring your own book to a place like this. But this Library is mainly for theologians and philosophers, so there's not too much fiction about. And if you're only here for a day or two, you can't read a book in that length of time, can you?"

She peered at Penny who did not seem to be listening to her.

"Penny? Did you talk to him? Did you talk to Gareth?"

"I did. We had a bit of a chat and then he got a phone call and had to leave. However, after talking it through with you, I do have some clarity and know what I must do. I have to be honest with him and tell him that I don't see marriage in our future. As you suggested, I have to be very clear about it so I don't lead him on. And then it'll be up to him what he wants to do when he knows how I really feel."

"I'm sorry to hear that, Penny. Thomas and I had such high hopes for you and him. We really wanted to see you get together. I suppose that's us being hopeless old romantics. And then there are the practical considerations. He will retire on a pension that would see you comfortable for the rest of your days, and many women would view that kind of financial stability as a huge attraction. In marrying him you might also be entitled to British citizenship, if that appealed to you. Still, you must do what is in your heart and what is right for both of you and in the end, being honest with him is probably for the best. I'm sure it will all work out. It will be what it's meant to be."

Penny sighed and stood up. "I hope so. I do feel better now that I've got some clarity on my feelings. I was a bit confused for a while there." She stood up. "Right. I'll be back about eleven thirty, I reckon. See you in a couple of hours and we can talk about what we want to do for lunch."

A couple of hours later, after a long thoughtful walk, Penny stepped through the gate that led from the Hawarden parkland, crossed over the A550 motorway and turned toward the small stretch of road called Gladstone Way, directly in front of the Library's main entrance. A small group had gathered on the pavement as if waiting for the arrival of an important personage or a passing parade. When she got closer, she recognized all the conference attendees, bundled up in coats and hats against a north wind which had turned surprisingly cold for this time of year. She joined the group and planted herself between Davies and Bronwyn.

He smiled down at her. "Good walk?"

She nodded. "What's all this? What's happening?"

"Minty's body is being moved to the local funeral home. The bishop wanted everyone from the conference to come out and pay their respects because they probably won't all be able to attend the funeral."

A moment later a black hearse drove into view, making

its way slowly down the street. The little group's heads all turned in unison to watch its approach and as it neared the bishop removed his hat and bowed his head slightly. His wife stared straight ahead, with an inscrutable expression on her face.

As the hearse approached, Reverend Shipton, who was staring at a small mobile telephone device in his hand, let out a low chuckle.

"Well, really," muttered Mrs. Lloyd. "Some people."

The hearse drove past and in its wake, the group broke up. The bishop and his wife said their good-byes and made their way up the path directly to the car park. The rest of the group straggled back toward the Library's main entrance.

"I'll be heading over to Colwyn Bay now," Davies said. "There's masses of paperwork waiting there for me. You'll be all right to go home with Mrs. Lloyd and Florence?"

Penny nodded. "I've still got some packing to do, but yes, I'll be fine." She hesitated. "I'm sorry for the way our getaway turned out. With us. I know it wasn't what you wanted."

"It's all right," Davies said. "I understand. Really. It's early days, as relationships go and taking things slow is just fine with me. But you'll find I'm a very patient guy. And no matter what happens, we'll always be friends."

"Of course we will. There's nothing I'd like more," said Penny. She watched as he followed in the bishop's footsteps to the car park.

"So, Penny, you're coming home on the train with us," said Mrs. Lloyd. "I suppose we'll have to take a taxi to the station as that policeman of yours has more important things to do than make sure we get there safely." She turned to

126

Florence. "Honestly, Florence, I was that shocked when that horrid little man started to laugh. I simply couldn't believe it. Whatever happened to old-fashioned manners and behaving in a respectful fashion?"

"I guess he's never heard the old saying," Florence said glumly.

"What old saying?"

"Never laugh as a hearse goes by, or you will be the next to die."

Twenty-one

*F*lorence and Mrs. Lloyd stood in the hall near the reception area, while Penny spoke to the receptionist. A moment later, she joined them.

"The taxi'll be here in thirty minutes," she said, "so that's plenty of time. I've got a bit of packing to do and then I thought I'd spend a few minutes in the Library before we go. I didn't see as much of it as I should have. I'll have to come back another time, I guess."

"That suits me," said Florence. "I'm all packed. I'll be in the Gladstone Room skimming the newspapers. What about you, Evelyn? Coming with me?"

"Yes, I suppose so." Mrs. Lloyd trudged after her, pausing to examine a print of William Gladstone and Queen Victoria having what looked like a one-sided conversation.

Penny returned to her room. With Thomas and Bronwyn

at the conference, and with the uncertainty of the depth and nature of her feelings for Davies, she had not felt comfortable to share a room with him, and they had agreed to take separate rooms. She folded the last of her clothes and placed them in her small suitcase. She checked the bathroom to make sure nothing had been left behind and after one last look around, closed the door behind her.

At the bottom of the stairs she tucked her suitcase out of the way and walked down the hall to the Library. She pulled open the heavy oak door and stepped into a quiet, book-filled world of learning and contemplation. The sun pouring in through leaded windows lit up the room, highlighting alcoves and niches that had not been so discernable the night before.

The library's main chamber, with its soaring, vaulted cathedral ceiling, was built on two levels. The ground floor housed books on religion. The second level, open in the centre, ranged like a minstrels' gallery around all four sides of the room, with a narrow spiral wooden staircase leading up to it. The room gave off a faint hint of the distinctive, remarkable smell of old books that is neither pleasant nor unpleasant—a combination of paper ageing over a very long time and slight dampness with a weak underlay of mustiness. After breathing the Library air for a few moments, Penny no longer noticed the smell.

Penny had always loved libraries. In the midst of a dysfunctional, burdened childhood she had found solace and escape in books, and the first place she had ever gone on her own was the small public library in the Nova Scotia town where she grew up. Walking along the summer streets in ugly, ill-fitting hand-me-down shoes as an emotionally neglected seven-year-old girl, clutching two Dr. Doolittle books under her arm, she navigated her way through the streets, retracing the route she had been shown two weeks earlier. She handed the books to the woman at the returns desk and wandered into the children's section, drinking in the bright colours of children's art displayed on the walls. For most people, a library is the introduction to a world of books and reading. For Penny, those had been just a delightful side effect. For her, the library had been the place where she discovered who she was and who she was meant to be. She had discovered the world of art when a kindly librarian noticed her examining the children's drawings on the walls and asked if she would like to come to the special art classes, held every Saturday morning. Penny nodded shyly and the librarian then showed her the selection of books in the adult section dedicated to art history.

And now, decades later, she nodded at another librarian, this one seated just inside the great oak door. She walked slowly down the length of the magnificent room gazing up at its great ribbed roof, like a giant, overturned rowboat. Turning her attention to the shelves, she ran her fingers along a few of the titles on the spines of the books: *Bird Life of the Bible, God: A Biography, The First Book of Samuel, Prophecy and Religion.*

She sat in one of the brown leather chairs in the main reading room and after admiring the carved oak columns that supported the upper gallery, her artist's eye followed the vertical lines of the library to the shelves of colourful books on the next level. You could never duplicate this with a digital collection, she thought. The warmth and richness of this beautiful place was in complete harmony with the priceless knowledge it contained. And the ecclesiastical look and atmosphere complemented perfectly the subject matter of the books. She climbed the stairs to the upper level, making her ascent on the narrow, well lit, spiral staircase holding the stout rope handrail. The upper level was filled with tall bookshelves in a warm, medium brown oak, arranged not in straight lines, but in clusters of niches and alcoves. Interspersed amongst the group of shelves strategically placed beside leaded windows to catch the light, were reading tables, each with a gooseneck brass lamp with an opaque glass shade.

Penny paused in front of a shelf in the history of the church section and moved on. She pulled off the shelf a small volume in dark green leather with raised bands on the spine cover and opened it. Entitled *Baxter's Works,* volume 8, it displayed a W. E. Gladstone bookplate on the front inside endpaper. This must be one of the original Gladstone books, she thought, admiring the colourful swirling pattern in bright yellow, red, and blue on the endpaper that carried over as marbled edges of the text block. She sighed and replaced it on the shelf.

Lost for a moment in simply examining it as a beautiful object, she realized she didn't know how long she'd been here. Twenty minutes? Time to think about getting back downstairs to meet up with Mrs. Lloyd and Florence.

She was grateful for these quiet moments to prepare herself for the train journey with Mrs. Lloyd. Florence wouldn't be a problem, but Mrs. Lloyd, with her comments and questions, was another matter. She sometimes asked the nosiest question imaginable and then ended with, "Or is that none of my business?" And when told that in fact it was none of her business, she accepted the response in good part, with a smile and a "well, I tried" kind of shrug.

Penny hoped they could get through the journey without Mrs. Lloyd making a sly reference to "that policeman of yours." He's a policeman, all right, and a lovely one at that, Penny thought. But is he my policeman?

And then the unexpectedly loud clang of a heavy door closing startled her. She frowned and turned her head in the direction she thought the sound had come from, somewhere behind her and over to her left. She could see nothing in all directions but more bookshelves and tables overlooking the ground floor. She peered over the railing and saw only the librarian seated at her desk, gently leafing through a large volume.

She took a step back from the shelf and only then noticed a small, red trickle beginning to pool on the polished oak floor. She peered around the end of the nearest bookcase.

A pale, watery beam of late morning sun filtered through the high window, casting a weak, forlorn shaft of light on the carrel tucked in beside the shelving unit. It bathed the still figure of Reverend Nigel Shipton, slumped over the small oak writing table, his back to the shelf of books below the window behind him. He was facing the gallery railing that overlooked the main floor below.

Swallowing, Penny took a tentative step towards him. She touched his shoulder and gave him a gentle shake, then recoiled in horror as a long hissing breath escaped from his lungs through pale blue lips. Dark blood was seeping from a long slash down the side of his coat. Instinctively she reached out her hand to stop the blood, then pulled it back,

133

curling her fingers into her palm and placing her closed fist on her chest. She took a step back and scrabbled about in her bag for her phone. She then took the bottom of Shipton's tweedy sports jacket and held it over the gaping hole in his coat.

A few moments later she leaned over the railing and in a normal speaking voice, told the librarian to summon the warden. The librarian looked up at her and placed a finger over her lips and made a shushing sound.

"We need help! Call 999 and then get the warden!" Someone's badly hurt.

"What happend?"

"Please," Penny repeated, "just get the warden. Now."

The librarian reached for her phone and a few moments later Graham Fletcher pushed open the Library's main door. He exchanged a few whispered words with the librarian at her desk and then following her pointing finger, raised his head toward Penny. She made a little beckoning hand gesture and he hurried up the spiral staircase. She met him at the top and spoke to him in a low voice.

"You're to close the Library now. No one is to be allowed in."

"Why?" demanded the warden. "Who says I'm to close the library? Really, this is just not on."

"DCI Davies says the Library is to be closed. He's called an ambulance. There's a body. At least I think it's a body. I'm pretty sure he's dead." She tipped her head slightly. "Over there."

"Oh, dear Lord, no," whispered the warden, covering his mouth with his hand. "Not another one. This is a disaster." He peered in the direction Penny indicated. "Who is it? Do we know?" and then he asked again, "What happened?"

"Well, it's Reverend Shipton and I'd say he's been stabbed. There's no knife, though. At least I didn't see one."

"No," breathed the warden, closing his eyes and rubbing his hand over this forehead "A body in Gladstone's Library. It's just not possible. This is just too awful for words." He thought for a moment. "I expect the place will be overrun with those forensics people and everyone will have to be interviewed all over again."

"Yes," replied Penny. "It's all going to be terribly inconvenient for you, I'm afraid. There'll be police everywhere you look."

The warden thought for a moment.

"But what about you? I heard you were just about to leave. A taxi had been called for you. Will you be allowed to go now?" he asked.

"No," said Penny. "I've been asked to stay until DCI Davies gets here. But would you please go to the Gladstone Room and tell the two ladies waiting in there that I've been delayed and I'll make my own way home later. Tell them it's okay for them to leave. But don't tell them about this." She gestured in the direction of her grisly find. The warden nodded. "Perhaps I should just have a look?" he asked. "Just to make sure, that, well, you know."

"The police want as few people as possible in here. That's why you have to close the Library. Except for the paramedics and police, of course."

At that moment the downstairs door opened and Florence

135

crept in. She whispered to the librarian, who pointed up to the gallery. Florence raised a worried face.

"The taxi's probably here and they're wondering what's happened to me," Penny whispered to the warden. "Please. Go down now and speak to her. Otherwise, they'll miss their train and believe me, you don't want Mrs. Lloyd hanging about with all this going on." The warden clattered down the stairs and a moment later said something to Florence. Her eyes widened and she then left the room, followed a moment later by the librarian and warden, leaving Penny alone in the great, silent expanse.

Twenty-two

"D idn't go so well, then."

Penny shook her head and groaned. "Two deaths and a semi-break up." Penny took a sip of her coffee. "Not really a break up, but I told him I want to continue as we are. For now. After all, we haven't even been going out for a year, so what's the rush? I need to sort out how I feel, although I think it's becoming clear to me. And if things aren't moving along fast enough to suit some people, that's their tough luck. Things were a little awkward for a bit, but he said he understands and he's okay with it. At least, I think he is. Well, I hope he is."

Victoria Hopkirk passed Penny a plate with two croissants on it. Penny shook her head, and Victoria took one for herself and tore it in half. Flaky crumbs dropped to her plate. She set half down and dabbed some raspberry conserve on the other half. The two friends were having breakfast together in Victoria's flat the day after Penny returned from Gladstone's Library.

"He's more into you than you're into him right now, that's all. That can change."

"You could put it like that, I suppose." Penny sighed. "I think he's hoping my feelings will change but I'm not so sure they will. Anyway, I don't want to talk about it anymore. It was good I didn't take the train home with Mrs. Lloyd and Florence. I don't think I could have handled her questions or going on about Gareth or as she likes to call him, 'that nice policeman of yours.' Not yours, mine. Well, you know what I mean."

"Let's get back to the body. What happened after you found the body in the Library?"

"Gareth asked me to hold the fort until the police arrived, which they did very soon and I gave a statement and came home on a later train."

"So there were two murders in two days?"

Penny nodded. "Two days. Felt like much longer than that." She smiled. "Is there any more orange juice?"

Victoria went to the kitchen and returned a moment later with a carton that she set down rather noisily on the table. She then pushed it toward Penny.

"Here. Help yourself. And don't change the subject. You know I'm desperate to hear all about the murders so off you go, and don't leave anything out."

Penny poured herself a second small glass of juice, drained it and then licked her lips.

"Well, let's see. First there was Minty Russell, the bishop's secretary. She was deathly allergic to seafood and somehow it seems there was some on her lunch plate, lurking in the chicken korma, and it made her very ill. It was frightening to see an allergic reaction. Even worse than what the symptoms did to her body was the panic and fear in her eyes. She knew what was happening to her, all right. Anyway, Bronwyn and Gareth jumped up and tried to help. They tore through her bag, but the device she needed to inject herself with was missing. It wasn't in her room, either, so that naturally made Gareth suspicious."

"Naturally. Go on."

"Well, she was taken to the hospital in Chester, where she died. We were told about it later that afternoon. Dinner was a pretty somber affair, I can tell you. And I suggested to Gareth that Florence might be able to translate Minty's shorthand notes—she used to be a secretary at the Liverpool College of Art, remember?—so she arrived in the late afternoon with Mrs. Lloyd in tow. But nothing turned up in the notebook.

"And then the next day, I found Reverend Shipton stabbed to death in the library. I get the feeling that nobody liked him very much, but nevertheless it was really awful seeing him like that."

"I bet it was. I've never understood how somebody could stab another person. You'd have to be so close to your victim and surely you'd feel the knife blade going in, cutting through the person's body." Victoria made an overhand stabbing gesture and grimaced.

"And if the attack were particularly vicious the person gets stabbed again and again." Penny shuddered. "But this was just the one entry wound, apparently. With a knife taken from the kitchen, possibly, but the police are still trying to find out where the knife came from."

"So who would have access to the kitchen?"

"Well, that's a good question. The police will be investigating every aspect of it," said Penny, "including interviewing all the kitchen staff. Again. They had to speak to everyone after Minty died. And, I guess they'll have to speak to everyone else who works there."

Victoria thought for a moment. "I'm curious about something. Let's say you had a thought, or remembered something, would you ring Gareth and tell him? Would you be comfortable doing that?"

"Of course," said Penny. "Why wouldn't I? He'd be one hundred percent professional. He's a policeman first. They always are."

"And what about that phone call that made you want to attend this conference in the first place?" Victoria asked. "Did you find out anything more about that? Did you tell him about it?"

Penny shook her head. "I never got around to mentioning it to him. In fact, I'd almost forgotten about it until I overheard two people talking." She thought for a moment. "They were in the Robinson Room and the man said practically the same thing as on the message. He called her darling and said they'd have to be careful. And then the people came out of the room and you'll never guess who they were."

"No, I probably won't, so you'd better tell me."

"It was the bishop's wife and the accountant."

"Pull the other one! Bishop's wives don't have affairs and even if she did, who'd have an affair with an accountant?"

Penny stood up. "I know. That's what I thought. But he's quite good-looking and well dressed. There's definitely something about him, but he's a little too smooth for my taste, if you know what I mean. I didn't get a chance to talk to him though, so what do I know?"

"What's his name?"

"Hywel Stephens."

"Stephens. Stephens. We have a Mrs. Stephens as one of our clients. I wonder it that's his wife." She turned to her computer and pulled up a program that listed all the clients of the Llanelen Spa. "Yes, here we are. Ros Stephens. She's, let me see, thirty-four." Victoria peered at Penny. Would that be about the right age for his wife?" Penny nodded. "Could be. I'd put him in his late thirties. Good-looking and well dressed, or did I already say that?"

"You did," said Victoria. "In fact, we almost had him as our accountant."

"We did?"

"Yes. When we were setting up our business the lawyer recommended a couple of accountants, including Stephens. And then Mrs. Lloyd also recommended him because his father, who started the firm, looked after her husband's fruit-and-vegetable business for years. And he must have done a good job because Mrs. Lloyd is comfortably well off and the Stephens's family firm has always done her accounts. They've seen her right."

"So did you contact him?" Penny asked. "Why isn't he our accountant, then?"

"I did contact him, but he wasn't available. His office said he handles a lot of work for British ex-pats in Spain and travels there often. So he wasn't available just when we needed him, so we went with someone else."

"I see."

"Most of his clients are corporate, I believe, but from what Mrs. Lloyd said, as a favour to her he continues to look after her personal finances. Because of the relationship with her husband and his father, I guess."

"And apparently he also looks after the accounting for the diocese," said Penny. "You don't think of churches as being the kind of organizations that would need insurance and legal and accounting services, but I guess they are."

"Well, they do have assets and money, payrolls and outgoing expenses, like every other organization."

"Hmm. Something to think about. Anyway, thanks for giving me breakfast. Best get on." Penny rubbed her hands together. "Oh, that reminds me. My poor, rough, dry, chapped hands. I could use some of Dilys's magic hand cream. I meant to ask, how are you getting on with the hand cream licensing?"

"Well, that didn't go so well, either." Victoria glanced at Penny. "The papers were all ready to sign, but Dilys didn't turn up. We're hoping she's just gone walkabout and will turn up in a day or two. I didn't want to bother you with that while you were at the Library. You had enough on your plate, I thought."

Penny frowned. "What do you mean Dilys didn't turn up? Did you go up to her cottage to see if she's okay? She's getting on. She might have fallen."

"Take it easy. I asked Emyr to check up on her. He went

down to her cottage, had a look round, and said everything seemed in order but there was no sign of her. He had no idea if anything was missing. So we're just going to wait and see and hope she turns up."

"Wait and see! Hope she turns up!" Penny reached for her phone.

"Who are you ringing?"

"Gareth."

"You can't ring him over this."

"Just watch me."

A moment later Penny pressed the button on her mobile to end the call and put the phone back in her bag.

"He's going to send someone to look into it." She frowned at her friend. "I must say I'm a little surprised that you didn't do more." She settled back in her chair. "Oh, I know what it is. You just don't like Dilys very much, do you?"

Victoria shook her head. "No, I don't. There's something about her I don't trust."

After living away for many years, Dilys Hughes, now in her seventies, had returned to Llanelen a few months ago when her brother had become ill. Although the brother had died, Emyr Gruffydd, the local landowner, had allowed Dilys to stay on in her brother's tied cottage while plans were completed and planning permission obtained to convert the cottages on his property into holiday lets.

Dilys's hands were remarkably youthful and although she always wore gloves to protect them from the sun, she had also been caring for them for decades with a special botanical cream she made herself. She would not sell the formula to Penny and Victoria for their new spa line, but had agreed, after much coaxing and negotiating, and the women suspected, after taking sound legal advice, to license the rights to the product to the Llanelen Spa for production as a private-label product.

"What concerns me," said Penny, "is that she stood to make a lot of money from this deal we offered her. So why would she not sign the papers? Emyr's not going to let her stay in the cottage for much longer and she's going to need a place to live. The money from this hand-cream deal could provide her with a nice little income."

"I wondered about that," said Victoria. "I thought perhaps she found the legalities too complicated and overwhelming and decided to just ignore it. People deal with things in different ways. And you know what she's like. She comes and goes. She's probably off somewhere and when she's good and ready, she'll come back."

"Well, we'll see if the police turn up anything." Penny checked her watch. "I keep thinking about Minty Russell. The look on her face. There was something else in there with the fear, too. Disbelief? Surprise?" She shook her head. "I can't put my finger on it, but it was almost as if . . . as if . . ."

"As if what?"

"I don't know. Almost as if she was surprised, but not completely, if you know what I mean."

"No, I don't really."

"And then, oh, I didn't really explain the part about the notebook properly. She had a shorthand notebook that Gareth thought might contain something important, so he asked Florence to come to the Library and translate it."

"Did she find anything interesting or useful?"

"No, that's the thing. It's what wasn't there that's interesting." Victoria raised a well-shaped eyebrow. "And what was that?"

"We don't know, do we, because it wasn't there. But some pages had been torn out of the notebook and Gareth would very much like to know what's on them."

"I guess he looked in all the usual places. Her handbag, room, flat, office, desk, and so on?"

"Yes, they've all been searched and so far nothing."

"Well, if she hid them at the Library, it might be easy enough to find them."

"What do you mean?"

Victoria responded with another question. "Well, think about it. Where's the best place to hide something?"

Penny tilted her head.

"Group like with like, of course," said Victoria with a hint of triumph in her voice. "Let's say for example, I had a bottle of rare and precious nail varnish, if there is such a thing. Where would I hide it?" Penny thought for a moment.

"On our shelves with all our nail varnish?"

"Exactly. No one would take any notice."

"So you're saying that if Minty wanted to hide the pages from her notebook, she'd probably hide them . . ."

"If the police have searched everywhere else for them, then one of two things must have happened. Either she threw them out or she hid them in the Library. And if she hid them in the Library, she probably hid them . . ."

"Between the pages of a book," said Penny. "Great. Now we've narrowed it down to, oh, 250,000 or so volumes."

Victoria shook her head. "No, it's much smaller than that. Think about it. Let's assume she wrote the notes in short-hand, then she could have hidden the pages in a shorthand book. But if she didn't, then you've got to find out if she borrowed any books from the Library while she was there." She raised her hands and then opened them in an expansive gesture.

"Hmm. Well, you've certainly given me something to think about." She stood up. "I'd best get on. Lots of e-mails to get through." As she stepped into the corridor, Rhian, the receptionist, handed her a slip of pink paper. "It's a phone message, Penny," she said, pointing at it. "She'd like you to call her." Penny glanced at the message: CALL BRONWYN ASAP.

Half an hour later Penny waved good-bye to Rhian and pushed open the door of the Spa. A warm breeze gently rippled the surface of the River Conwy, and she paused for a moment to enjoy the way it sparkled in the spring sunshine. She crossed the town's famous three-arched Inigo Jones bridge and arrived at the Ivy teashop. The doorway was low and she almost had to duck as she entered. When her eyes adjusted to the lower light, she spotted Bronwyn waiting for her at a corner table.

"I know you're probably busy, Penny, after being away for a few days, so I'm very glad you were free to meet me for lunch." Penny slipped off her jacket and sat down. Bronwyn smiled as the server placed menus on the table and then retreated.

"What is it, Bronwyn?" Penny asked. "You look worried. Is everything all right? It's not Robbie, is it?"

Bronwyn laughed lightly and her face lit up the way it always did at the mention of Robbie's name. "No, Robbie's fine, but I was that happy to see him again after our time away, I can tell you." She settled back into her seat. "Let's order first and then I'll explain."

They studied the menus and then Penny looked at Bronwyn and raised an eyebrow. "Do you know what you're having?" Bronwyn nodded as the server arrived to take their orders. After she had left, Bronwyn folded her hands on the table and leaned forward.

"I wanted to talk to you, Penny, because Thomas has had a very worrying e-mail from Graham Fletcher. You know, our old friend the warden at Gladstone's Library," Bronwyn began.

Penny nodded. "Yes, I know who he is."

"Right, well, we didn't get to spend as much time with him as we would have liked, because he was new in his job and working and then those two dreadful things happened. Minty Russell and Reverend Shipton. We understand that. But in the past couple of days Thomas has been getting the most worrying e-mails from Graham. They're long and ranting. We can't even always make sense of them. All about how he worked so hard to get the post and how angry he is that Shipton had to go and get himself killed in the Library and cause him, Graham that is, so much bother. And he thought the police had wound up the Minty investigation and things could get back to normal and now they're back. And how the bishop has it in for him now and thinks he killed Minty Russell. We think poor Graham is going off the deep end and we're terribly concerned about him. But what's really bothering us is his saying the bishop thinks he killed Minty."

She paused while the server placed a Welsh rarebit with

a small side salad in front of each woman. They picked up their forks and attacked the delicious melted cheese with Welsh mustard oozing off a thick slice of bread from the local bakery.

"Mmm," said Penny. "Heavenly. Sorry, Bronwyn, you were saying . . ."

"Yes, we're worried about our friend Graham and what he said about the bishop thinking he killed Minty Russell. We don't know why he would say that, and I wondered if, oh I know if Gareth did say anything to you it would have been in confidence, and I do hate to ask, but I wondered if Gareth had said anything to you that you felt you could share with me about suspects in the case? Is it true, do you know, that the police suspect Graham?"

Penny poked at a tomato slice. "Gareth hasn't said anything to me. He's always very discreet and professional about his cases and doesn't tell me anything that isn't generally known. It's the way police officers are at his level. They just keep things to themselves and bottle it all up, even though doing that can cause problems at home."

"The thing is, Thomas and I don't know what to do for the best. We hadn't seen Graham in years, but at one time we were all great friends so I suppose we feel some sense of loyalty to the friendship that used to be." She hesitated, took a sip of water and then took the plunge.

"We wondered, Thomas and I, if you would consider going back to the Library to try to find out what's going on. I know it's a lot to ask, but if Graham is a suspect, we think you might be able to help him." She opened her handbag. "Thomas printed out Graham's e-mails so you can read them for yourself. He rambles on dreadfully, as I said, but there might be something in there amongst all the ranting."

Penny protested: "But Bronwyn, the police will get to the bottom of this. They'll find out what happened."

"Yes, but we're afraid it'll take too long," Bronwyn replied. "Graham seems very fragile and we thought if you could get a faster result, then his mind could be at rest. To be honest, we're afraid that he might, well, do something to hurt himself."

She gave Penny a pleading look that spoke volumes about her concern. "He couldn't have done anything to Minty; he's just not that kind of person. We're sure of it."

Twenty-three

A single return to Chester, please."

"The train's on the platform now and leaving in four minutes. You can just make it if you get your skates on." The railway agent handed over two orange tickets.

Penny hurried along the platform and climbed into the first carriage. Because Llandudno is the first or last station on the line, depending on which direction you're travelling, the carriage was almost empty. Penny squeezed down the narrow aisle and chose a forward-facing window seat in a configuration of four—two seats facing forward, two facing backward, with a table between them. She set her overnight case on the seat beside her and as the train pulled out of the station, opened a notebook on the table, and drew a line down the centre. At the top of the page on the right she wrote MINTY RUSSELL and on left she wrote SHIPTON.

Her pen hovered over the page. She scratched her cheek with her other hand and drew lines down the page with the headings MEANS, MOTIVE, and OPPORTUNITY at the top. She made a few notations, but she finally put the pen down and looked out the window. The train was slowing down as it approached Llandudno Junction.

Well, that's something, she thought. I know absolutely nothing about either of them, except that they both worked for the Church in Wales. What a daft exercise this is. What could I possibly discover at the Library that the police, with their expertise and resources, had not or could not? She hoped Davies was doing better with his investigation.

The front door to Gladstone's Library beckoned as Penny walked up the same pathway Minty Russell had just a few days earlier. As she passed the ornate bronze statue of William Gladstone that stood in the front grounds, she paused to take a closer look. At its base were three figures representing classical learning, finance, eloquence, and one playing an Irish harp. The monument had been created by Irish sculptor John Hughes to be erected in Dublin, but when the city council refused to accept it, it had been donated to the Library in the 1920s. So for the last nine decades, a sober, dour Gladstone, clad in the flowing robes of a Roman senator which he had probably never worn in life but were so beloved of sculptors, had gazed steadily over the stone wall covered in greenery and the metal fence that separated the Library's front lawn from Gladstone Way.

Penny entered the now familiar reception area of the

Library and had a quick word with the receptionist. As she accepted her key, Warden Graham Fletcher approached her.

Penny was taken aback by the change in his appearance in just a few days. Dark rings circled his dull, vacant eyes and he seemed wreathed in despair and desolation. His shoulders hunched into his jacket and the loose skin on his noticeably thinner face drooped into sad little jowls.

"Ah, Miss Brannigan," he said. "So good to have you back with us. I do hope your stay this time will be much more uneventful."

"Yes," agreed Penny. "So do I."

"Now, do let me know if there's anything you need or anything I can do to make your visit more comfortable," the warden said.

"Thank you," said Penny. "I'm just going to take my case upstairs and then I'm going to browse in the Library. Unfortunately, I didn't spend nearly as much time there as I should have on my last visit. I'm here to remedy that now."

"Well, here, let me help you," said the warden, reaching for her overnight case and turning toward the stairs that led to the bedroom level.

"Oh, that's very kind of you," said Penny. And I hope I can help you, Penny thought. Bronwyn had assured her that Thomas would not mention to the warden the real purpose of her visit.

Fletcher led the way.

"Have the police finished here?" Penny asked when they reached the landing that looked out over the garden statuary.

"They seem to have wrapped up the forensics part, but the man in charge told us they could return at any time to ask more questions or reinterview us." He let out a little sigh. "Such a dreadful business. I'm sure nothing like that has ever happened here before." He smiled at Penny. "But our beautiful Library is open again, so that's some consolation." He set the suitcase down outside the door of a single room at the end of the corridor. "Well, it only remains for me to wish you a pleasant stay. If you should need me for anything at all, my office is just down the hall there, at the end." He pointed toward the Library wing.

"My office is just adjacent to the Library chamber," said the warden. "It's never far from my thoughts and I am never far from it. Literally."

"Oh, right, well, thank you," said Penny. "I see I have a couple of hours before dinner, so I must use that time wisely."

She opened the door and let herself into the comfortable, modern room that was oddly made even more comfortable by its lack of a television set, standard in a hotel room.

As part of the Library's mission of creating an environment conducive to quiet contemplation—thinking and reading—there were no in-room distractions. Anyway, they weren't needed, as anyone staying in the Library could sign out any book from the Library or borrow any book from the Gladstone Room's collection of contemporary fiction. And the people who chose to stay here were usually involved in research or writing projects that took up all their time and attention.

Penny set down her suitcase and approached the leaded

window that offered a view of the fence and graveyard of St. Deiniol's Church, which was adjacent to the Library. She unfastened the latch, pushed the window open, and stuck out her head. A clatter below caught her attention, and she looked down. A kitchen worker dumped a large plastic bucket filled with potato peelings, eggshells, carrot scrapings, and other kitchen waste into a large, green composting bin, closed the lid, and disappeared from view, presumably back into the kitchen.

Penny pulled her head back in. She washed her hands, collected a pen and notebook, and headed downstairs to the Library.

The librarian, a young woman in her late twenties with fair, shoulder-length hair, looked up and smiled as Penny entered. She was not the same one who had been on duty the day Penny discovered Shipton's body.

"Hello," Penny said in a whispery voice. The librarian acknowledged the greeting with a slight nod but said nothing. "I wonder if you can help me," Penny continued. "Is it possible to check what books someone signed out?" The librarian looked at her warily.

"Why would you want to know that?"

"I'm looking for a piece of paper and it might be in a book that was signed out by someone who was staying here a few days ago." The librarian maintained her steady, questioning expression so Penny smiled and changed tack. "How does the sign-out system work?"

"It's simple. You find the book you want and then you fill out one of the tickets and counterfoils in the booklets scattered all over the Library." She showed Penny a simple form with write-in space for the name of the book and name and room number of the borrower. "You take the book you want off the shelf and leave the ticket in the spot where the book was. Leave the counterfoil in the booklet. When you bring the book back, you leave it here." She gestured at a small stack of books at one end of her desk. "And when the book is reshelved, we take the ticket. Don't reshelve the books yourself."

"It seems like a very trusting system," said Penny.

"Yes, you'd think that," agreed the librarian, "but very few of our books ever go missing. I guess that's because many of the people who use the Library are clergy and the concept of thou shalt not steal is something they're very familiar with."

"One would hope so," said Penny. "Now these forms that you collect when the book is reshelved. Keep them for a bit, do you?"

"For a bit."

"Then I wonder if you'd be kind enough to tell me what book or books Minty Russell signed out. She was here earlier. She organized the Church in Wales conference that was held here."

"Oh, I'm afraid I couldn't do that. It's a privacy issue, you see."

"Yes, of course."

"Russell, Russell," the librarian said. "Isn't that the lady who was taken ill here and then . . ."

"Yes," said Penny. "Sadly, she died." Penny swallowed and took a deep breath. "You see, she was working on a project that was very dear to her and I have undertaken to finish it for her, in her memory, as it were, so it would be helpful if I knew what books she was reading at the time. I believe she checked out at least one book from the Library."

The librarian thought for a moment and then opened a drawer and took out a small sheaf of paper tickets. She flipped through them and pulled two.

"Here we are. Seems she was interested in the plight of the Victorian servant and also a history of middle-class English Victorian women who travelled out to India." She took off her glasses and ran her hand over her eyes, then replaced the glasses. "I know that book. Fascinating. They went out either to marry army officers or work as governesses." She jotted down the call numbers of the books on the back of a small scrap of recycled paper and handed it to Penny.

"Where can I find them?" asked Penny.

"In the history section. Upper level, top of the stairs, on the left." Penny looked up at the second tier and pointed above their heads. "Over there?"

The librarian nodded. It was not far from the table where she had discovered Shipton's body. An uncomfortable tension seemed to connect the two women as if each was wondering whether to mention the body in the library. But the moment passed. Penny nodded her thanks and climbed the stairs to the gallery.

She compared the numbers on the slip of paper to the numbers on the spines of the books, looking for a match. When she came to the two books Minty Russell had checked out, she hesitated. She had an uncomfortable feeling she was crossing over into police territory. Would Gareth be upset if she handled these books, possibly destroying fingerprints, if the piece of paper she was searching for was within their pages? But the librarians have already handled the books, she told herself. She pulled them off the shelf and took them to a small side table. But not the table where Shipton's body had been.

She opened the first book and thumbed through the pages, then held the book upside down by the cover. The pages fanned out, but nothing fell from them. She closed the book and set it on the table and did the same with the second. Again, nothing. She let out a small sound of frustrated disappointment that was somewhere between a sigh and a hiss. She'd been so sure she'd find the missing page or pages from Minty Russell's shorthand notebook.

She went back to the first book and examined it more closely, running her fingers down the cover and checking to see if anything had been tucked in anywhere. Again, nothing. After doing the same with the second book, she admitted defeat and returned to the ground floor and placed the books in the return pile.

Well, what now, she wondered. There was just enough time for a mind-clearing walk before dinner, so she returned to her room to fetch her jacket and let herself out the front door. She walked down the path and turned left, toward neighbouring St. Deiniol's Church. After exploring the churchyard, with its tipsy tombstones and statuary covered in smooth green lichen, and examining signs listing the types of birds and trees to be found in the area, she turned back toward the Library. She glanced up at her window, which overlooked the church, and then hearing a noise from the other side of the stone wall that separated the Library from the church, entered the gate, and walked through the area where the rubbish and composting bins were located. Obviously the kitchen area, she thought, taking in the sign that said DELIVERIES with an arrow. She looked up again at the window of her room. Below it was a window that must be part of the kitchen suite. A small chalkboard, easily seen from the area in which she was standing, had been set up inside the window. FOUR CREAM, TWO REGULAR, TWO SKIM, had been written on it. That's efficient, she thought. The kitchen staff write their daily order on the chalkboard in letters large enough so the milkman can read the message without having to leave his delivery vehicle so he only has to make the one trip.

She walked on and turned left, which brought her to the rear of the building. She sat down on the bench marked JUSTICE and thought about the blackboard she had just seen in the kitchen window. Old fashioned and low tech, for sure, but efficient and effective. Is there another blackboard in the kitchen, she wondered. One that the person in charge of the kitchen could use to communicate instructions to the staff? To list the next day's menu perhaps? Or, possibly, to note if a particular guest had a specific allergy? To nuts, say? Or seafood?

She got to her feet and walked round to the front of the building and entered by the main door.

A few minutes later she closed the door to her room, sat on the bed, and got out her laptop. When it was up and running, she tried to access her e-mail but the Wi-Fi reception was poor. She took her computer down the hall and set it on the window ledge outside the Robinson Room, where it worked perfectly.

She read a few messages, answered some, and deleted a

couple. Then, she opened a message from Victoria with the subject line CONWY CASTLE.

Lord Chamberlain's Men performing *Macbeth* at the castle in August, Penny read. Tickets go fast. Ordering six. We'll make up a party.

Great, Penny typed in reply. *Macbeth* is my favourite play. Thought that group just did the comedies but look forward to it. She finished her e-mailing, closed her laptop and returned to her room. It was 6:45 P.M. and dinner service was starting, but she lay down on her bed, opened a book, and began to read. Twenty minutes later, when she judged that most, if not all of the guests, would have been served, she went downstairs and entered the dining room. As she had hoped there was no queue. The menu board listed a choice of lamb hotpot, grilled salmon fillet, and a vegetarian risotto as that evening's entree choices.

She smiled as she approached the server and gestured. "I'd like the grilled salmon, please." The server picked up a spatula from the metal tray containing the salmon and placed a fillet on a plate, added rice and vegetables, and handed the plate to Penny.

"I guess you have to use a separate utensil with the salmon," Penny remarked.

"Yes," the server said. "Some people are allergic to fish. And other things. We have to be careful."

"So if a guest lets you know that she's allergic to something, is the kitchen staff informed?" Penny asked.

"Sometimes," the server said. "But we're always very careful with our ingredients and our utensils. Same with vegetarian and non-vegetarian. We can't stir a pot with meat in it—a stew, say, and then use the same spoon to stir a vegetarian dish. We can't transfer anything. We just assume allergies and always take precautions. You can't be too careful."

"Makes sense," said Penny. "Well, thank you."

"I'm just about to end service, so if you want pudding, you'd better take it now. It's apple crumble. Homemade, of course."

Penny indicated she wanted some and the server spooned it into a small bowl and added a generous ladle of custard. The server checked her watch and then leaned over to see if anyone was behind Penny. Seeing no one, she reached up and pulled down the metal grille. When it was halfway down, she paused.

"Is there anything else?" she asked Penny, who had not moved.

"I'm sorry," said Penny, "but I'm curious. I always like to know how things work. When I was out walking I noticed the sign you have for the milk delivery and I wondered . . . how would the kitchen staff be informed about an allergy?"

The server's eyes narrowed slightly. "That's a funny question for you to be asking."

"Is it?"

"Do you have an allergy?"

"No, I don't, but I know someone who has and she was thinking about coming here to stay with me, so I just wanted to make sure that a food allergy wouldn't be a problem for you or for her."

"No, not a problem. We've had a lot of experience with them. Your friend will be fine here." She pulled the grille down the rest of the way with a loud clatter and locked it into place, leaving Penny to enter the dining room.

The warden was sitting by himself at the back of the room, a plate of uneaten vegetables cooling in front of him. Penny approached his table and set her tray down. "Good evening, Warden Fletcher," she said, "I wondered if I might . . ."

Fletcher made a small, slight gesture of pushing the plate away from him, and then turned his gaze upward. Penny gave a short, sharp intake of breath.

She set her tray down and then sank into the chair beside him.

"Warden . . . Warden Fletcher," she began, "are you ill?"

He shook his head. "Oh, it's you again. I'm sorry, forgive me, I've forgotten your name."

"It's Penny Brannigan. I was here at the conference as a guest speaker. I'm the one who found Reverend Shipton's body. And we met again a few hours ago. You were kind enough to show me to my room."

"Yes, I do remember that you were at the conference, although some details are fuzzy to me. It's just with all this upset I haven't been sleeping." He made an airy, vague gesture, then a wringing motion with his hands. "First, the terrible things that happened, and then all the police activity, roaming about and asking endless questions, although thankfully that seems to be winding down now." He took a sip of water. Penny lifted her plate from the tray and propped the tray between her chair and the table leg. "I heard earlier today that the funeral for Miss Russell is going ahead," the warden said. "I haven't heard what's happening with Shipton. At least Miss Russell has family. Poor old Shipton just has a, well, companion, I guess you'd call him, and apparently he's disappeared. But really, what would anyone expect? The fellow may not even have been in the country legally, for all we know. Came from Nigeria, I believe."

"Warden, I'd like to ask you a question about that if you don't mind. At the opening night party, Miss Russell was instructed to tell Shipton that his companion had to leave. Do you know if he did leave or did he stay here?"

The warden shook his head. "I have no idea. I don't know what happened to him, but I didn't see him again. So if he was here, he made himself scarce."

"Bronwyn Evans told me that the three of you used to be great friends at university—you and Thomas and Bronwyn. They had so been looking forward to seeing you again."

"Yes, we'd lost touch, rather, over the past few years, and I had just e-mailed Thomas to let them know that I had been awarded this living," the warden said. "Sorry, that's old-fashioned church talk . . . I had just been offered and accepted this position." He sighed. "I had such high hopes, and then these terrible things had to happen."

"But surely once everything is sorted and things get back to normal you'll be able to carry on," Penny said. "After all, nobody's blaming you."

"Aren't they?" asked the warden. "Two deaths happened on my watch and I hear the bishop's not best pleased."

"Has he contacted you?" Penny asked. "Has he said anything to you?"

The warden did not reply and a few moments later excused himself.

Twenty-four

After dinner, Penny wrote a long e-mail to Davies describing the warden's changed and alarming appearance. His remark about the bishop bothered her. No doubt Davies had been speaking to the bishop and she wondered what, if anything, he'd turned up.

Half an hour later, she received a reply from him. The investigation was ongoing and he had nothing he could share with her and hoped she'd understand. She knew what that meant and she did understand. The investigation might very well have turned up something interesting, but as the senior investigating officer, he meant what he said. He could not share anything with her. She had come to accept that this was not a reflection on her or his trust in her, it was just how police worked.

She browsed the bookshelves in the Gladstone Room, found a novel that appealed to her, and decided to take it to her room. There was definitely something to be said about leaving worldly materialism behind and spending a few quiet days enjoying the simple pleasures of a slower-paced life: walking, reading, napping, and thinking. Simple, delicious meals featuring old-fashioned British favourites were prepared from scratch and served at regular times without fuss and bother. I could get used to this, she thought. This must be what it's like to live in a monastery or another closed community.

She returned to her room, settled in for the night, read a few pages, and then turned out the light.

A few hours later she was awakened by a loud banging, vibrating sound coming from the pipes in the en suite bathroom. After a moment, the juddering stopped. The joys of elderly plumbing, she thought. The room was dark, and she had no idea what time it was. She switched on the bedside lamp and checked her watch. Just gone half past two. She was wide awake and knew she wouldn't be able to get back to sleep for some time. This happened to her occasionally and she found that the best use of her time was to do something productive so she got out of bed, put on her dressing gown and slippers, and picked up her laptop.

She opened the door. Her room was at the end of one corridor, with the warden's office at the opposite end and another corridor running east and west past her door. The corridor was dimly lit and deathly quiet. She stepped out into the hall and, making sure she had her room key in her dressing gown pocket, closed the door quietly behind her.

She was about halfway down the hall on her way to the

Robinson Room when a small noise behind her made her turn. In the muted light she caught a glimpse of a figure she thought was a man. A moment later it disappeared from view down the corridor that led past her door. She was sure it was the warden, but what was he doing roaming the corridors so late at night?

She opened the door to the Robinson Room, the same room where she had presented her talk just a few days ago on the work of architect Owen Jones to the women attending the conference. Sitting at the end of the table she logged into the Wi-Fi and began to check her e-mails. After deleting the ones that didn't interest her, she opened a rather long one from Davies and two short ones from Victoria. In the first one, Victoria confirmed that she had been able to get tickets for *Macbeth* and in the second one, she said there was still no sign of Dilys, so the licensing rights for the new hand cream hadn't been sorted. Penny pondered that for a moment, not sure how to respond. What on earth was going on there?

She looked up from her computer and her eyes roamed the room. Across from her were floor to ceiling bookshelves that stretched the length of the room. She wondered if the bookshelves contained overflow books from the Library's main collection, and stood up to browse the titles. They were catalogued and part of the Library collection, and appeared to be a comprehensive collection of biblical philosophy texts, with titles such as *Mission in the New Testament* and *The Origin of Christology*. On closer examination, she realized these shelves held the archives, correspondence, and library of Dr. John Robinson, who had been Bishop of Woolwich and Dean of Trinity College, Cambridge.

On one end of the shelves, behind the door, were small

storage boxes that held his personal papers. Alongside these were books he had written and even a bound edition of his Ph.D. thesis.

She ran her hands along the boxes at eye level noting the contents listed. Box 26 intrigued her. The contents on the spine were listed as Clare College Chapel Letters, Trinity College Chapel Letters, Sex. She opened it to find a series of stiff pamphlets from Clare College and Trinity College, dating from 1951 to 1983. The only thing relating to sex was a yellow booklet entitled *The Place of Law in the Field of Sex,* written by The Rt. Rev. John A. T. Robinson. She reached for Box 28, labeled Miscellaneous and Unknown Correspondence, Cancer, and The John Robinson Memorial Fund. As she pulled the box from the shelf a piece of paper that had been wedged between it and Box 29 fluttered to the floor. She picked it up and, with her heart beginning to beat faster, unfolded it.

It was lined, with a vertical orientation and at the top were jagged edges where it had been ripped from a coil-bound notebook.

Written in pencil were three initials and numbers with pound signs in front of them and question marks after them.

PB £80?
GF £40?
S £100?

It's got to be one of the missing pages from Minty Russell's steno book, she thought. And then she remembered that on the morning of her presentation, Minty had paused for a moment behind the door before coming out into the corridor. Had she spent that moment tucking this piece of paper between the storage boxes intending to retrieve it later? It looks like the same kind of paper in her shorthand notebook, but what does it mean? Penny turned the paper over. There was nothing written on the back. Sitting at the table, she mulled over the numbers. Were they amounts owed her? But if so, she would know how much she was owed and wouldn't be questioning the number. Two of the initials seemed obvious—PB stood for Pamela Blaine and GF for Graham Fletcher. But the S puzzled her. Shipton? Stephens? Somebody else?

She refolded the paper and tucked it in the pocket of her dressing gown. After a moment, she returned to her laptop and began to type a message to Davies. She hoped she'd hear back from him before morning. An hour later she was awakened by the ping of a text message on her phone.

This is what I'd like you do, his message began. It ended with him saying he and PC Chris Jones would be with her just after breakfast.

Twenty-five

*D*avies's instructions had been very clear—she must find a way to speak to Warden Graham Fletcher in his office. So at just past nine, Penny knocked on the half-open door.

He looked even worse than he had yesterday, the cumulative effect of another sleepless night. As he rubbed his hands together in a scrubbing motion, she detected a faint trembling. As if sensing her watching him, he then locked his hands together and placed them in his lap.

"What can I do for you?" he asked. His eyes flicked in her direction and then focused on the papers in front of him.

"Well, I just wanted to offer to give a lecture or talk at some time in the future," Penny began. "I know you encourage writers to come here and speak, but I wondered if you've thought about having an artist? The presentation I did at the conference on the work of Owen Jones was rather well received, I thought. There are so many statues of William Gladstone dotted about—including the magnificent one out front of the Library, so I thought a presentation on Gladstone statues might make for an interesting evening."

The warden brightened a little. "Indeed it might. Perhaps if you could let me have a written proposal, a brief outline of what your talk might include and when you think you might be able to do this? We're booked into the summer now, but possibly late summer or early autumn?"

"That would be wonderful," Penny said. "I'll do that." She rose a little from her chair and then sank down again.

"Oh, I wondered if you'd heard. Apparently there's been a major development in the Minty Russell case."

Fletcher peered at her through cloudy brown eyes and leaned slightly forward as he fingered the knot on his tie.

"Oh, no, I hadn't heard. What's happened?"

"Well, it seems they've found Miss Russell's EpiPen. You know, the medical device she needed to inject herself with that they couldn't find when she was having the allergic reaction." As Davies told her to do, Penny watched the warden's eyes intently. There was an almost imperceptible widening, the tiniest of frowns, and his eyes looked down and slightly to the right. A microsecond later, he raised them to meet hers.

"Yes, they found one in her office, so it may be that she didn't have one with her after all."

"Then would that mean . . . ?"

"Well, it could mean that her death was a tragic accident. Her plate could have got contaminated somehow. It's easy enough to understand how that could have happened, despite all the precautions in place. A busy server would just have had to use the wrong utensil, one that had been in contact with seafood, because there was fish on the menu that day, and then used that same utensil to put something on Miss Russell's plate."

"So the police think it was an accident, then?" he asked.

"Maybe. I don't know, really. You'd have to ask them that." As a silence settled over them, Penny's eyes swept the warden's office. The bookshelves were almost empty except for a few books lying on their sides that looked as if they had been carelessly set down. On her left was a thick metal double door painted bright orange. It was propped open slightly. Both sides were fitted with heavy locks with large oval hand pulls that disengaged the bolting mechanism.

"That door, warden," she started to ask.

"Yes," he interrupted, "I know what you're about to say. That door looks so out of keeping with the rest of the place. And you'd be right. It's a fire door. It's solid metal, but it's been disguised on the other side to fit in with the overall look of the Library. It's supposed to be kept shut at all times because if the building ever caught fire we would want to do everything we could to prevent it spreading into the Library. But I like to keep the door open just a little so I can breathe the Library air. Now, if you'll excuse me, I'm a little behind in my preparations for an important meeting with the trustees this afternoon." He checked his watch and then stood up.

"Yes, sorry, terribly sorry but I've just remembered something I've got to do." Penny opened the door that led to the corridor, and then sprinted down the hall to her

173

room where Davies was waiting for her. Together, they walked to the window and looked out.

"You were right," Penny said. "As soon as I mentioned it, his behaviour changed."

"We shouldn't have long to wait," Davies said. He picked up his cell phone and pressed a button. "Everybody in position and stand by."

A few moments later, the warden appeared below their window. "He's come out of the kitchen," Penny said. "The kitchen door is right below this window." The warden looked around him and then, in a few quick strides, reached the rubbish bin parked against the stone wall that separated the kitchen area from the churchyard next door. He opened the lid and dropped something in just as a figure emerged from the right. The warden looked startled and then relaxed and smiled as the council bin man, dressed in a navy blue uniform with a high-visibility jacket, reached out for the bin.

Penny leaned forward to try to get a closer look at the bin man and then pointed at him. "Wait. That's Chris. Chris Jones. That constable I like."

"It is," smiled Davies. "And he's going to check the bin and . . ." He stopped to answer his phone. "Yes, all right. Got it. Good. Thanks."

He turned to Penny. "Chris just picked up the EpiPen. It wasn't in the bin when he photographed it a few minutes ago, so we know the warden dropped it in. We'll have him doing that on CCTV as well. The EpiPen will be tested for fingerprints to make sure it's Minty Russell's, but I'm confident we'll get the result we expect."

He tipped his head. "Right, well, time to talk to the warden and listen to what he has to say."

"May I come?"

Davies gave her a wry look. "I think you know the answer to that. You go downstairs and have a coffee, and I'll join you in the Gladstone Room as soon as I can." He was about to say something else when a knock on the door interrupted him. Davies nodded at Penny and made a little gesture toward the door. She opened it to find Chris Jones, changed out of his bin-man uniform and looking every inch a police officer.

"Coming, Jones," Davies said. He turned back to Penny and repeated himself. "Wait downstairs. I'll join you when this is over." He took a couple of steps and then turned back.

"Why did you suspect him?" he asked.

"I realized his odd behaviour wasn't because of his concern for the Library or what the bishop thought. It was guilt, pure and simple," she said.

"Guilt?"

"The sleepwalking, hand wringing . . ."

Davies raised an eyebrow.

"Lady Macbeth."

Twenty-six

The warden looked up in surprise as Gareth Davies entered his office.

"Good morning, warden. I'm afraid we've come to talk to you on a serious matter." PC Chris Jones followed him into the room, holding a small notebook in one hand and a carrier bag in the other.

The warden looked from one to the other.

"Yes," he said. "I was half expecting you. There seems to be no end to this. Please sit down, both of you."

"I want to talk to you about the death of Minty Russell," Davies began. "We interviewed you before, but in light of new developments, we need to talk to you again, and this time I want you to tell me everything you know about it."

The warden's eyes shifted to Jones, who remained standing, and then back to Davies.

"You want me to tell you everything I know about the death of the bishop's secretary? I hardly knew the woman. She organized the conference that was held here, but until then, I'd never met her. We spoke a couple of times about conference arrangements but other than that . . ." He shrugged. "Sadly, while she was here she had an allergic food reaction. But was the food necessarily from our kitchen? Perhaps she ate something she had purchased somewhere else. Really, that's about it. I don't know how I can help you or what more I can tell you. I've told you everything. Several times, in fact." He shifted uneasily in his chair. "I was told this morning that you, that is the police, now think her unfortunate demise was accidental. Is that not correct?"

Davies nodded at Jones, who removed a plastic evidence bag from the carrier bag. He handed it to Davies, who placed it on Fletcher's desk and carefully smoothed it out so the warden could see the contents clearly.

"This is an EpiPen we recovered from the rubbish bin in the Library kitchen area about ten minutes ago. We saw you put it in the bin and you were photographed doing that. Now I'd like you to tell me how you came to have it in your possession."

The warden's shoulders sank as he sighed and leaned forward. He closed his eyes and his whole body went limp.

"I don't know if I should say anything," he said, finally.

"That's entirely up to you. We can have a chat here or we can go to the police station in Buckley where I will place you under arrest, and at that time you'll be cautioned and interviewed by trained officers. That's the neat, tidy, official way of doing things and Jones and I are just fine with that, aren't we Jones?"

Jones nodded. "We are, sir."

"She wanted money," Fletcher said in a low voice.

"How much money?" Davies asked.

"Not a lot," Fletcher said. "Forty pounds a week, was what she said. But then she added, 'to start'. So I knew it would never end, that she'd always be holding it over me."

"Holding what over you?"

"I lied on my CV. I said I'd finished a masters degree in divinity at Oxford. She checked my references and called my old college. She found out I hadn't finished my thesis and that the degree was never granted. But for some reason she told the bishop everything was in order and he approved my application as warden of this beautiful place." He raised a hand and gestured toward the Library on the other side of the orange metal door. "This cathedral of books." Fletcher's eyes filled with tears as a haunted, painful silence filled the room.

"It was all I ever wanted," Fletcher continued. "For thirty years I wanted this living, to live here and to be surrounded by all this beauty. And then she . . ." His voice broke and a choking sob caught in his throat.

"When did she present her offer?" Davies asked.

"On the first day of the conference, while we were having morning coffee in the Gladstone Room." He raised his eyes to Davies and gave a derisive laugh. "After you had given your presentation. Oh, she was very coy. She said she knew about my master's degree and that I could trust her not to say anything to the bishop. That she was sure we

179

could come to a suitable arrangement. It was all very subtle, but there was no doubt what she was doing and what she was after."

"And then what?"

"She said she'd give me some time to think about it and we'd talk again. So I went through the rest of the morning with that hanging over me. She was going to ruin me. I felt I had no choice but to get rid of her."

"And how did you do that?" Davies asked.

"I saw the notice on the board in the kitchen about her food allergy and it was easy to get some salmon paste. The kitchen staff had been very careful with her food. They're very good with allergies, and I'm sorry they've been implicated in this. It had nothing to do with them. I smeared the paste on some pieces of chicken. Anybody who tasted it wouldn't have noticed it. It was about the same colour as the korma sauce. I didn't know her allergy was that bad. I thought it would just make her sick and she'd have to go home and it would buy me some time to think. I wasn't thinking straight. I couldn't think what to do or how to get myself out of the mess."

"Did you consider talking to the bishop and maybe offering to finish the thesis?" Davies asked.

"You must be joking. Have you spoken to him? He's the coldest, most unforgiving person you could possibly imagine." The warden spat out the words. "Talk to him?" Fletcher let out a snort of disdain. "Don't make me laugh."

"So how did you get the EpiPen out of her bag?"

"Oh, that was easy. She left her bag hanging on the back of her chair. I stopped by the table to ask if everything was all right and just took it. It was in a side pouch. I figured she'd keep it where she had easy access to it. After all, when you need something like that, you can't waste time messing about looking for it, the way you and Bronwyn were."

Fletcher thought for a moment. "Anyway, after I took the EpiPen, at that point I told myself it's not too late, you don't have to go through with this. But I felt myself caught up in something. It was almost as if something had been set in motion, something quite apart from myself, something I wasn't controlling."

A slow smile started to spread across his face.

"You know, I feel strangely better." He put both hands on his shoulders, palms facing upward, and raised them. "Lighter. As if a terrible burden has been lifted from me. Well, they do say confession is good for the soul."

He looked at Davies and let out a long, slow breath.

"I never knew anyone who was murdered and I never knew anyone who had killed someone. I always wondered what kind of person, an ordinary person, could kill someone. What forces would drive them to it? How would they feel afterwards? Could they live with themselves? And would it be worth it?" He placed his hands on the desk, one of top of the other. "And now I'm about to discover the answers to all those questions."

Davies nodded. "Yes, you are."

"But before you ask, Inspector, I didn't kill that swine Shipton," Fletcher said, his voice rising. "You've got to believe me. I didn't kill Shipton. I was as appalled as everyone else. Maybe even more so."

"No," agreed Davies. "I don't think you did have any-thing to do with Shipton's murder. Your murder was simple and rather sloppy, if you don't mind me saying so. You had no idea how bad her allergy was and how much or how little salmon paste would be needed to kill her. Very hit and miss. If her allergy had been less severe, then perhaps you would only have succeeded in making her ill.

"Your murder was not very well thought through. Any-way, someone once said that murder is for amateurs and killing is for professionals. Take poor Shipton, for example. Someone much more ruthless and cunning than you did for him. His murder was clinical. But tell me. You called him a swine. Why?"

"Because that's exactly what he was. Everybody loathed him, especially the bishop. I heard that Blaine was get-ting ready to ask the archbishop to move Shipton to another diocese in another part of the country. Wanted to wash his hands of him. Couldn't stand him. And then Shipton went and got himself killed, saving him a lot of bother."

"What was the problem with Shipton? Why did the bishop dislike him so much?"

"He was a thorn in his side. Unmanageable. Thought the rules didn't apply to him. Never handed anything in on time. Sloppy recordkeeping. The bishop is a real stickler for that sort of thing. Lives by process, does the bishop. Shipton just couldn't be bothered. Took great pride in con-sidering himself a rule breaker, but everyone just consid-ered him a loose cannon."

"How do you know this?"

Fletcher rubbed his red, swollen eyes. "All the rectors

know it. It's been going on for years. One wonders why the bishop put up with it as long as he did. I don't even think Shipton was particularly religious. No idea why he went into the church. It's not as if anyone has to, nowadays." He let out a mournful, resigned sigh. "What happens now? About me, I mean?"

"I shall caution you and you'll be taken in for questioning."

"I expect I'll go to prison."

Davies gave a tight nod. "Yes, you probably will. Murder usually involves a custodial sentence."

Fletcher took one last, longing look around his office, with its bare shelves still waiting for his books that would now never be displayed, and then stood up. "Right, well. I suppose this is when you put the handcuffs on me?"

"I don't think that will be necessary, do you?" said Davies, as the three prepared to leave. "I expect you'll come quietly like the gentleman you are." He nodded at Jones, who opened the door.

"But I can't help feeling all this has been such a shame," Davies said. "Two lives destroyed. One lost and another in ruins. And in the end, for what? For nothing."

With the warden placed in the back of a police car, Davies joined Penny. He found her gazing out a window of the Gladstone Room with its unobstructed view of the front entrance.

She turned to face him. "So he's gone." Davies nodded. "I don't know how I'm going to tell Bronwyn," Penny said.

"You don't have to," Davies replied. "I'll do it. I've had lots of practice delivering bad news."

Penny sat down in one of the brown leather chairs and Davies sat near her. "So what happens now?" Penny asked.

"The warden's just given me some interesting information that means we can open a new line of inquiry. And we're going to use it to find out who killed Shipton."

Twenty-seven

"Where do we start?" asked Penny.

"We?" he asked, with a wry smile.

"Well, you're the one who used the word 'we', so naturally I thought you meant us. Anyway, I'm here now, so I might as well be useful," Penny replied.

"Very well. Let's start with this." Davies unfolded the note Penny had found in the Robinson Room with the three initials and amounts that she'd given to him earlier.

"Fletcher confirmed that Minty Russell was attempting to blackmail him, and this," he said pointing at the list, "is exactly the amount she was asking for. So let's assume she was also trying to blackmail the others on the list for these amounts. So PB here is Pamela Blaine. Minty thought she was good for eighty pounds. But who does the *S* stand for? Shipton?"

"Stephens?"

"Unfortunately, Shipton's dead so we can't talk to him. But it's more likely Minty had something on him, and we need to find out what that was."

"His boyfriend?" Penny asked.

"Sexual behaviour used to be first-rate grounds for blackmail, back in the cold war days, but not anymore. These days, homosexuality, adultery. . . . Who cares?

"Let's consider Shipton as the *S* on Minty's list. The boyfriend could factor into this. There could be something in his ethnicity."

Davies flipped through the pages in his notebook. "Mr. Azumi Odogwu, he's called. He may be in this country illegally and we'll certainly ask our friends in the UK Border Agency to do a workup on him. We'll also see if they have a landing address for him. We've been through Shipton's residence, but there's no sign of Mr. Odogwu."

"Do we know where he lived?" Penny asked. "Well, Shipton lived in Abergele, so it's likely Odogwu is or was also living there," Davies replied. "We'll find him, sooner rather than later, I hope. But the warden told me something interesting about Shipton. Said the bishop positively loathed him."

"Did he say why?"

"He was difficult to manage and paid absolutely no attention to his paperwork."

Penny laughed. "I'm sure there were times when the bishop said, 'I could kill that Shipton,' but he didn't mean it. You don't kill someone because they didn't get the paperwork done on time. Otherwise, Victoria would have killed me ages ago. She's always complaining how hard it is to keep on top of her monthly reports because I don't submit receipts or expense claims on time."

Davies stood up. "Let's go back to the Library and have a look at the desk Shipton was working at when you found him. See if it jogs any memories for you, besides the obvious one."

They walked silently down the corridor to the Library and up the stairs to the table where Penny had found Shipton.

"I remember that the scene was so jarring because of the contrasts." Penny gestured at the table. "I don't know if this is the same table or not," she said, rubbing the edge of the table with the tips of her fingers, "but when I found him, on one hand, there was the gentle appearance of someone working in a library." She glanced up at him. "You know. Two or three books. A few papers on the desk, a couple of pens, some paperclips, I think. And just here," she pointed to a specific place on the table, "were his glasses. He'd taken off his glasses and set them down on the desk. And in the middle of all this normalcy was his body, with blood seeping out of it. It was such a contrast between what you'd expect to find in a library and the last thing you'd expect to find." She pursed her lips as if about to whistle and let out a long, slow breath. "But also, on the disruptive side, if you will, there were a few pieces of paper on the floor, too, as if someone had disturbed his papers."

After one last look around, they returned to the Gladstone Room.

"Well?" Penny asked.

"I'm going to drive you to Llandudno, where I'm meeting Bethan, and we're going on to interview the bishop and his wife. You'll be all right to make your own way home from there?"

Penny nodded. "Yes, that'll be fine. I'll just go and pack."

Penny gazed out the window of the automobile as green fields dotted with ewes and their newborn lambs flew by. Something at the edge of her mind, trying to creep out from the shadowy underbrush of nothingness into the light of realization, was toying with her consciousness. Whatever it was, she could not bring it into focus and make it meaningful. Was it something she'd seen on the table where Shipton had died? Was there something different about something ordinary? She let out a long sigh. Davies took his eyes off the road for a moment and glanced at her.

"All right?"

She nodded. "Yes. I'm fine." She pushed the image or idea she was struggling to retrieve to the back of her mind, knowing it would present itself when she least expected it.

Twenty-eight

"Really, Pamela. Must we have all this drama now?" The bishop set down his teacup and fixed his wife with a cold blue eye. "The police are on their way here with more questions, the archbishop is deeply concerned about all the negative publicity the deaths at the Library are attracting and, in case you hadn't noticed, I'm missing a secretary." He gestured through his open office door at the desk formerly used by Minty, upon which unopened letters, parcels, leaflets, files, and other documents were piling up. "I have no idea what to do with any of that," the bishop said, "I don't like the way this place is looking. If the archbishop dropped in, as he very well might, he would find the office in a completely unacceptable state. I can't go on like this. I must arrange for a replacement as quickly as possible."

"Michael, would you just listen to yourself? Minty has

died. She was murdered. And all you can do is go on about how messy your office is looking and moaning because you don't have a secretary. Well, poor you. Could you be any more self-centred?"

The bishop looked surprised and shocked.

"I'm sorry you're having such a hard time of it, Michael," his wife continued, her tone hard and laced with sarcasm, "and I'm sorry to add to your troubles at this time, but I can't take any more of this, either. I've been unhappy for a long time. I never really wanted to marry you, you know. But first you talked me into it, and then my mother wouldn't let me change my mind. She knew you were going places and was so ambitious for me." She shook her head. "I was so young, I didn't know how to say no. To you or to her. But everything would have been so much better for both of us if I had just said no. I was never cut out for this kind of life." She gave an unhappy sort of laugh. "It's too bad, really. You could have found yourself someone really good, who would have given you all the support you needed. Some meek little thing who would've seen looking after you and telling you how wonderful you are her life's work. Someone who would've been good at it and found it rewarding. There are, after all, advantages to being a bishop's wife, I suppose, if you're cut out for that sort of thing. Which I am not." She glanced out the window at the trees in their bright new foliage and then back at her husband. "Do you know, riding in the car with my father on the way to the church to marry you, I knew I was making a terrible mistake. I just wish I could have told someone who would've listened to me. We would have both been so much happier with other people." She paused. "And maybe it's not too late."

"What, exactly, are you saying, Pamela?"

"I just told you, Michael. I'm saying that I'm leaving you. I've had enough and I'm leaving. I don't want to live like this anymore. I can't live like this anymore."

"Please, Pamela. Don't. Don't do this. Don't go. Think about what it will look like, if you leave now while I'm in the midst of all this," he gestured helplessly around his office, "this chaos. Minty gone and police all over the place, asking the same questions over and over again." He stood up and walked around to the side of the desk where his wife remained seated. "Look, Pamela," he said in a softer tone, "I know I haven't been as attentive to you as I should have been and I'm sorry. But please, don't go. Not now. We can sort things out, I know we can."

"No, Michael, we can't. My mind's made up. This has been a long time coming." She stood up. "It's over. I realize now that what we've always had was a parent–child relationship. And what happens? The child grows up and leaves home. We were never equal partners in this marriage. At this point I should probably say I don't love you anymore but the thing is, I don't think I ever did. Not really. Not properly. Whatever love means."

She took a few steps toward the door before he caught her by the arm and swung her around to face him. She raised her arm and tried to pull away from him. "Let go of me. You're hurting me."

He released his grip. "Is there someone else?" he demanded.

She hesitated a fraction of a second too long before answering. "No."

"Who is it, Pamela?" he said, his voice trembling. "Tell me who it is."

She shook her head. "It doesn't matter. There was someone, but it's over."

"Pamela, I have a right to know. Tell me who it is." He said the words slowly, with a slight pause between them. She glared at him, pulled her arm away, and left the room. She strode past Minty's desk and did not look back.

The bishop returned to his desk and sat for a moment in shocked silence. A few minutes later he heard the front door close. And then he realized he had no idea where she was going.

Pamela Blaine got into her car and drove slowly away. She didn't know where she was going, either, but she felt a strange sense of elated relief, as if a burden she had been carrying for far too long had suddenly been lifted from her shoulders. She'd told him she was leaving, and she was. She drove slowly through the town until she came to a popular pub situated picturesquely beside the river. She got out of her car, went in, and ordered a glass of white wine. She paid, then took it to an empty table by the window and drained it in three or four gulps. Her hand shook a little as she set the glass down. She reached into her handbag and pulled out her mobile. She wrapped her hand tighter around it and left the pub. She walked round to the back and down to the river. In one smooth motion she flung the mobile into the gently flowing water, where it landed with a small splash and disappeared. "Good-bye to you, too, Hywel," she said. And then she got into her car and followed the signs to the motorway that led to Cardiff. She thought of the Beatles' song "She's Leaving Home" and laughed. "That's exactly what it is," she said. "I'm leaving home."

The bishop sat at his desk and stared unseeing at the papers in front of him. His thoughts were in turmoil as his mind darted from one thought to another, each one darker than the last. Where had she gone? Would she be back? Surely she'd be back as soon as she'd had a chance to calm down and think things through. And the affair. Who was it? Who had she had the affair with? He felt as if he'd been punched in the stomach.

He groaned as the doorbell rang. Not now, he thought. It rang again and with huge reluctance, he answered it.

"But I've already been interviewed and I've told you all I know. Everything." He glared at Davies and then stood back so the two police officers could enter. Best get them inside, away from the neighbours' prying eyes.

"Some new information has come to light. I'd like to ask you about your relationship with Reverend Shipton."

"Shipton? My relationship with him?"

"Yes. Did you like him?"

"Not particularly. But I didn't wish him dead and I certainly didn't kill him, if that's what you're asking. How could I have? My wife and I left the Library right after the hearse went by. We did not return to the building. I wasn't there. I'd gone home. Look, what's all this about?"

"I'm sorry to trouble you again, Bishop, but two people who work for you were murdered. I am investigating their deaths. If I may say, bishop, you don't seem to be as concerned about all this as I would have expected."

"Oh, I am concerned, inspector. Murder is a very bad thing. We don't approve of it at all in my line of work. You may recall we have a list of ten things we're commanded not to do and number six on that list is 'Thou shalt not kill.' And from an organizational point of view, murder tends to attract the wrong kind of publicity. And the archbishop has been on at me like you wouldn't believe. So for all kinds of reasons, I care very much about what's going on."

The bishop put his head in his hands and then slowly looked up at Davies.

"I'm sorry for that," he said in a resigned tone. "I don't mean to seem uncooperative. It's just that I'm having a terrible day. The worst in a very long time, to be honest. It's my wife, you see. She, well, let's just say there's been a bit of trouble on the domestic front."

"I'm sorry to hear that. You've all been under a lot of stress these past few days. Your wife here, is she?"

"No, she's, er, gone out. I'm expecting her back any time now." He then added, "I hope. She didn't take anything with her."

"She didn't take anything with her? What do you mean by that?"

"She drove off in her car, but she didn't take a suitcase or anything like that with her, so I expect she'll be back." He peered at Davies. "You don't need to talk to her, surely?"

"Yes, as a matter of fact, I do."

"What about?"

"I want to be able to eliminate her from our enquiry," Davies replied smoothly.

Davies looked around the bishop's tidy, uncluttered office and noted the stark contrast to Minty's workspace. Files were neatly stacked on a table but there were no photos. "We've had a look in Miss Russell's desk, as you know, but we're going to need to do another search."

"Search? In that case, I hope you've got a warrant."

"Yes, sir, we do. We'll be examining all phone records, parish reports, financial statements, everything. In fact, we'll be taking Miss Russell's computer with us."

"Wait a minute, Inspector. Exactly what are you looking for?"

When Davies did not reply, the bishop continued. "Just as I thought. You're fishing. You don't know what you're looking for, do you?"

"Bishop, we have two people dead. Murdered. Now quite often when two people who are connected in some way are murdered, the second murder was committed in an attempt to cover up the first. The second victim knows something and the killer believes he has to kill him, too. But in this case, we have two killers. The person who killed Minty Russell is not the same person who killed Reverend Shipton. So the murders are connected in some underlying, indirect way, because both people worked for you, but they are not connected to the extent that their deaths are the work of one person. Do you understand?"

"Yes, I think so," the bishop said slowly. "It's a lot to take in. But who killed Minty, then? Have you arrested someone?"

"We have," Davies replied, and told him who it was.

"I can't believe he would do such a thing," the bishop said. "Why would he do that?"

"We haven't finished interviewing him yet, but we should know more in a day or two," Davies said, reaching into his coat pocket. "But it seems he lied to you about his qualifications for the job, and Miss Russell knew that." He held out a piece of paper. "Here's that warrant you were asking about." He nodded at the police officers who accompanied him and, on his signal, they began disconnecting the components of Minty's computer. "If you'll just sign here, sir," Davies said a few minutes later. "We're leaving now, but we will be back. I'll have more questions for you, and I do want to speak to your wife." He handed the bishop his card. "If and when she returns, please ask her to call me." As Davies turned to leave, the bishop stood up. "Inspector, what you said about Miss Russell just reminded me of something. The first night of the conference, just as the opening drinks reception was about to get started, she came to me waving a piece of paper about and asking if she could have a word. Of course, it wasn't a good time—our guests were due any second—so I put her off. But I wonder now if what she had to say was important and connected to all this somehow."

"What did she want to talk to you about? What was on the paper, do you know? Did she leave it with you?"

"No, she didn't give it to me. I don't know what was on it, but it looked like numbers on a spreadsheet. I didn't get a close look at it."

Davies nodded. "Thank you for that. It might help when we're going through her computer files. We didn't find a piece of paper like that amongst her effects at the Library."

The bishop watched them leave, a worried frown creasing

his face making him look almost angry. When the door had closed behind them, he reached for his telephone and rang his wife's mobile. It went to voicemail. And then he thought about the seventh commandment—thou shalt not commit adultery—and took a deep breath.

Twenty-nine

*R*os Stephens picked a teddy bear off the sitting room floor and propped it against the back of the sofa. She plugged in the vacuum cleaner and hovered the carpet in long, straight strokes. At the jangling sound of something metallic being sucked into the hose, she sighed and switched it off. She'd lost or misplaced an earring from a set her husband had brought home to her from one of his business trips and, with a surge of happy relief, she thought she'd found it. She tipped out the dust cannister but instead of the earring she'd hoped and expected to find, she found a small key. She brushed a bit of carpet fluff off it and holding it between her thumb and forefinger peered at it. It didn't look like one of her keys. It wasn't a house or car key, it looked more like the key to a cabinet or desk. She walked down the hall, entered her husband's study, and pulled open the unlocked drawer to his desk. She tried to put the key in the drawer, but it didn't fit. She closed the drawer and turned her attention to the filing cabinet tucked behind the desk. She pulled on the top drawer; it did not budge, so she inserted the key in the lock. It fit. She left it there and returned to the living room. Although she rarely entered her husband's study, the fact that he had locked the filing cabinet began to bother her. Why would he do that? There were just the three of them in the house, and her six-year-old son, Tudur, would have no interest in the contents of an accountant's filing cabinet. So her husband must have locked it to prevent her from seeing what was inside.

As her curiosity increased, so did her anxiety. What could be in the cabinet that her husband did not want her to see? Was he keeping financial difficulties from her? She marched back to the study and opened the top drawer of the filing cabinet. It contained nothing but files. She closed the drawer and looked in the bottom drawer. It, too, was filled with files in different colored folders. She closed the drawer and went back to the top drawer. The tab on each folder was labeled in her husband's neat printing and arranged in alphabetical order. Using both hands she flipped through them, pausing occasionally to peer inside: American Express; Mobiles; Property; Visa. If she saw something that interested her, she pulled the file, set it on the desk and returned to the drawer.

When she'd been through the drawers, she sat in the desk chair and picked up the American Express file. She hadn't known he had an American Express card; she'd never seen him use it. She pulled out a statement and examined the charges; they seemed to be mainly for restaurant meals in Marbella, Spain. Well, that would make sense; his firm had several expatriate clients in Spain; he travelled there often on business and, in fact, that's where he was now. So the American Express card must be for business expenses.

She started to open the file labeled PROPERTY and paused for a moment to check the time on her mobile phone. She had a late afternoon appointment for a facial and manicure at the Llanelen Spa and didn't want to be late. Plenty of time. She turned back to the property file, expecting it to contain information on the modern two-storey home they owned in Llanelen. There were some papers relating to it, but the file also contained several documents in Spanish that she couldn't understand, but then she came to an estate agent's listing, in English, dated two years previously:

> Quick sale needed! Semidetached villa situated in a good residential area with twenty-four hour security and golf course. The house has three bedrooms (each with its own bathroom), living room, separate dining room, full-fitted kitchen, and a porch with garden access. West-facing views of the sea. The property also features extras such as air conditioning and heating, marble floors, fireplace, double glazing, electric shutters and covered parking.

Listing price was 400,000 euros. Why that was, she tapped a few numbers into her smart phone—326,000 pounds!

Stunned, she struggled to make sense of what she had

just read. Had Hywel actually bought an expensive property in Spain and not discussed it with her? How could he do that? Their own house here in Llanelen hadn't cost that much and, more to the point, this Spanish villa sounded much nicer. Three bedrooms, each with its own bathroom! And if he'd wanted to keep this purchase from her, why hadn't he kept the file in his office? She thought about that for a moment, and then the answer came to her. Because he couldn't lock the cabinet in his office. His PA would need access to the client files and it would seem strange to keep personal files at the office. But the American Express card with its business expenses. . . . She thought for a few more moments and then pressed a key on her mobile.

"Hello, Mum? I need you to come to the house and stop over for a night or two and look after Tudur." She listened for a moment. "Tomorrow. I've got a few things to sort out and I'll let you know. Right. I'll fill you in later. Got to go. Thanks, Mum."

Next, she booked a flight.

Thirty

*H*ello, Mrs. Stephens," said Penny, placing her client's fingers in a soaking bowl. "How are you? Enjoy the facial? Your skin looks very fresh." Ros Stephens smiled and nodded. "Did you have any particular nail varnish colour in mind today? Special occasion? Did you want your nails to match a particular outfit?"

"Well, something light and summery, perhaps. I'm going to Spain tomorrow."

"Oh, right," said Penny. She stood up and selected a few bottles from the display that her young assistant, Eirlys, kept so well-organized. "How about one of these? See anything here you like?" Ros pointed to a bottle of coral-coloured polish, and Penny set it aside. "So, Spain. Very nice. I expect it will be much warmer than it is here."

Ros nodded but did not reply. After putting the files

back in the cabinet, she'd tried to reach her husband but his mobile had gone straight to voice mail. As she thought about the property in Marbella, she wondered if he might have purchased it as an investment, and then, with the steep and sudden fall of the euro, and the disastrous decline of the Spanish economy, had been reluctant to tell her he'd bought it. She had read stories in the newspapers about British people who had invested every penny of their retirement nest eggs in Spanish properties only to see their value plummet by tens of thousands of euros. He was probably renting it out, but as the exchange rate was no longer favourable, it wouldn't be generating as much income.

And then again, Hywel might be staying in the villa instead of hotels when he went to Spain, she thought. He did seem to be spending more time out there. Perhaps he was picking up more clients in the expat communities in Malaga and Marbella. There were still quite a few Brits operating businesses—pubs, fish-and-chip shops, and the like.

"Yes, I expect it will be," Ros said. "Warmer out there. I must remember to pack the sunscreen."

Thirty-one

The foothills of the Sierra Blanca were browner than she expected, but no landscape could be as deeply green as the Welsh hills and valleys she had left behind. She peered out the window as the plane came in to land, and after clearing customs and collecting her suitcase, she stepped through the exit doors of Malaga-Costa del Sol airport into the welcome embrace of a wall of warm air. She accepted an offer from a waiting taxi driver and showed him a piece of paper on which she had written the address of the villa. He helped her put her bag in the car and under a bright blue sky, they drove off.

She gazed out the car window as they left the airport behind them, then drove along a motorway, past tall white apartment buildings that were shimmering in the sun. Palm trees waved at the side of the road, and not too far off, the

Mediterranean sparkled in the morning sunshine. About thirty minutes later, they turned off the main road and wound their way through a tidy subdivision of immaculately maintained houses. The driver stopped in front of one and said, "Here we are."

Ros got out of the car, thanked and paid the driver, and stood looking at the house as he drove off. Then, she picked up her suitcase and walked to the front door.

She knocked and waited. A moment later a dark-haired woman who appeared to be in her mid-thirties opened it. She wore a loose blouse, almost off the shoulders, a full skirt, and sandals. "*¿Sí?*" she said, with a small smile that revealed even, white teeth. "*¿Quién es, amorcita?*" said a male voice behind her. A moment later Ros was astonished to see her husband step into view, holding in his arms a little boy who looked the spit and image of her own son, Tudur, as he had looked about three years ago. As the blood drained from his face, Hywel handed the child to the woman and grabbed the door, trying to step outside and close it behind him just as Ros stepped over the threshold, her arms in front of her.

It's nice for him I had that manicure before I left Wales, she thought, as, filled with blind fury, she lashed out at him. Because these coral-red nails are the last things he's going to see before I claw his eyes out.

Thirty-two

O h, Penny," said an eager Mrs. Lloyd as she seated herself at the manicure table the next day. "You will not
believe what's happened. I can scarcely credit it myself but
I always thought there was something not quite on the up
and up with that Hywel Stephens. Not half the man his
father was, believe me.

"Anyway, it seems that he's got himself another family
out there in Spain." She settled deeper into the chair and
placed her hands on the white towel that covered the work
table. "Honestly, his poor wife is beside herself, still trying
to take it all in. She thought there was something funny
going on and went out there to see for herself. And what
does she find but him, playing happy families in a posh
villa in Marbella. He's got himself a fancy woman and
they've had a child together. Looks just like young Tudur,

according to Ros. And not only that, but to add insult to injury, the Spanish house cost more than hers did. That's what Ros told her mother."

Eyes glittering with excitement, Mrs. Lloyd gave Penny a look of triumph at having delivered this thrilling news, reminding her of an excited Mrs. Bennett in *Pride and Prejudice* bursting to share the latest newsy tidbit.

"I don't know what's going to happen now," Mrs. Lloyd continued, "but I wouldn't want to be in Hywel's shoes when he gets back here. And his business is here, so he'll have to come back and face the music sooner or later. He can't stay away forever. Ros was beyond furious, as you can imagine. Not to mention terribly hurt." Mrs. Lloyd dipped her fingers into the soaking bowl Penny had prepared and then pulled them out again. "Oh, Penny, you always get this water so hot. Eirlys gets it just right. Is she not here today? No offence, Penny, but I've rather come to prefer my manicures with her."

"I know you do, Mrs. Lloyd, and no offence taken. Whatever you want is fine with me. She's having a few days off, but she'll be back next week. Now, please, tell me more about the Stephens. I want to hear all about it."

"I bet you do." Mrs. Lloyd shook her head. "It's amazing, isn't it? You read about this sort of thing in the newspapers, but you never imagine that someone you know would get involved in such a scheme." She thought for a moment. "A long time ago—you probably won't remember this—but there was a film with Alec Guinness. He played a man who did the same thing. He was a sea captain who had an English wife, see, and their life together was all very cozy and staid, chintz on the furniture, afternoon tea and gardening, and a mug of cocoa in front of the fire, that sort of thing. But he also kept another wife across the Channel, a French or Spanish sexpot type of woman and when he was with her they'd go dancing and drinking and stay out until all hours, getting up to all sorts. I wonder if there was something like that going on here? I mean, you don't really think of an accountant as being one for the ladies, do you?"

"I'm that astonished, Mrs. Lloyd, I really don't know what to say." Penny dried Mrs. Lloyd's hand and began filing her nails. "And Ros was in here for a manicure just before she left for Spain, too. She told me she was going out there, but I doubt she was expecting to find that. It must have been awful for her."

"Well, now, of course, after all these years I'll have to find a new accountant. I couldn't possibly stay with him now. And if he loses his business, which he very well could, he'll have a hard time supporting one family, never mind two." Mrs. Lloyd put her hand back in the soaking bowl and Penny started shaping the nails on her other hand. "It must have cost him a pretty penny, Penny," she said with a sly smile, "to support two families and all the travel back and forth on top of it. It can't have been cheap. Besides juggling his time I expect he had to juggle his finances, too."

"Yes, I expect you're right as usual, Mrs. Lloyd," said Penny. She thought for a moment. "I wonder . . . If Ros didn't know about the Spanish family, do you think the Spanish woman knew about the Welsh family?"

"Hmm. I don't know. I expect we'll learn more details over the next few days. We'll have to be careful what we believe, though. There'll be a lot of gossip about this. It'll be the talk of the town for the next little while, that's for sure."

The two women were silent for a moment and then Penny asked, "Mrs. Lloyd, how did you hear about this?"

"Well, we live on the same street, don't we? And Ros's mother was looking after Tudur and she told me all about it."

"It makes you wonder, doesn't it?" said Victoria. "How someone could live a double life like that. He must have worn himself out trying to keep everything straight."

Penny laughed. "Most men have enough trouble getting on with one wife. Two seems a lot to take on. It must have been awful trying to remember every little detail. He must have been very clever not to mix the two women up. You know, how one likes her tea. Or, God forbid, call one by the other wife's name."

"Actually, I was reading a magazine article about adultery and how men get away with it," said Victoria. "One thing they do is never call the wife or the mistress by her name. It's always darling, or honey, or sweetie, or babe, or something like that. That way they don't get them mixed up. But was he actually married to both of them, I wonder, which would make him a bigamist, or just living with the Spanish one?"

"Mrs. Lloyd didn't say," said Penny. "But there are two children involved, and I suspect this will all get really messy. When it comes time to sort it all out legally, it's going to be ugly. I expect there'll be a divorce and all kinds of ramifications. And his business will likely suffer terribly. Mrs. Lloyd said she couldn't possibly continue to use him. But if he's an excellent accountant, which apparently he is, and she's done very well with him as her advisor for many years, it'll be too bad if she decides to take her business somewhere else."

"Well, speaking of legal, I've got papers here for you to sign. Dilys turned up a few days ago and finally gave us the formula for the hand cream, so her licensing agreement can go ahead. The arrangement is fair to everyone, I think." Victoria gave Penny a large envelope.

"You don't have to sign it now. Take it home and read it over."

"Good idea." Penny picked up the envelope and stuffed it in her bag.

"I've been thinking about this and I've got one request and one suggestion."

"Fire away."

"First, the laboratory where we get this made."

"There are several we can use."

"Right. I'd like to use one that does not do animal testing."

"I agree," said Victoria. "We're ethical."

"So that's my request and here's my suggestion. I thought about all the different kinds of fragrances it could be, and then I thought we should go with the simplest one of all."

"Lavender? You love lavender. Or lavender vanilla? That's very popular. Or maybe different fragrances?"

"No," said Penny. "No fragrance. Fragrance free. We've taken a real stand on the tanning-bed issue and I thought we could do the same with fragrance."

"That wasn't what I thought you were going to say. I'd

like to think about it, but my first reaction is that I like that idea very much. It might appeal to more people, too."

"Good. Where was Dilys, by the way? She'd gone missing and I've been so focused on what happened at the Library I haven't thought about her for days. Was she all right? Where was she?"

"She'd gone walkabout. She turned up again about two days ago. Emyr thinks she was sleeping rough. Apparently she likes to do that every now and again. Without a doubt, she is a very strange creature."

Thirty-three

*P*enny was tired and looking forward to spending a quiet evening at home with her feet up and her kitten, Harrison, now a gangly teenager, curled up on her lap. He had been rescued from a fire at Ty Brith Hall a few weeks earlier and given to her by the Hall's owner, Emyr Gruffydd. She'd always thought of herself as more of a dog person, but was finding the kitten an absolute joy to have around, and she looked forward to seeing him each day when she returned home. Besides, he was easier to manage than a dog.

She slipped her key in the lock and let herself into the picturesque cottage she had inherited from an old friend the previous year. She'd spent a considerable amount of money updating and renovating it, and loved the result. The cottage was warm, inviting, stylish and above all, hers. As she hung up her coat, a small grey figure walked toward her. She set down her bag and scooped him up into her arms.

A moment later they set off for the kitchen. "Well, I know what you're having for dinner," she said. "But what about me?"

When she had finished her microwaved meal, she plugged in the kettle and made a small pot of tea. She set this on the table and went to the hall to fetch her bag. She pulled out the contract Victoria had given her, poured a cup of tea, and sat down to read.

Twenty minutes later, bogged down in legal jargon and not really sure what she had read, she stood up, carried her cup to the kitchen, and set it in the sink. She walked through to the sitting room and sat down in a comfortable wing chair. She needed a few quiet moments to think.

Something Victoria had said during their chat had struck a chord. About how expensive it would have been for Hywel Stephens, a small-town accountant, albeit with some big clients, to run two households in two countries. Did he have that kind of money? Did he have access to it? Could he get it?

She poured herself a glass of white wine. Was it possible that Minty knew about the Spanish family? Hywel Stephens's initials—HS—weren't on Minty's blackmail list, but did the S stand for Stephens? Penny smiled at the irony. If Minty had known about the Spanish family, Stephens could have been the biggest and best blackmail target of all of them—the one with the most to protect and the most money to pay.

Everyone has secrets, she thought. And for all sorts of

reasons, people keep secrets for other people. Had someone in the Church in Wales been keeping this secret for Stephens? Had the bishop known about it? She snapped her fingers. Of course! Who was the most likely person to have known about the Spanish family? The bishop's wife. After all, she was having an affair with him. What if Stephens found the whole arrangement just too heavy a burden and in a moment that he would be deeply regretting now, confided the details of his double life to Pamela Blaine? Had Pamela then, in a pique of jealousy, tipped off Ros Stephens? What had prompted Ros to go off to Spain like that? Why now? And how had she known where to find Stephens, anyway? So many unanswered questions.

And what about poor old Shipton? Gareth had told her they were poking into every aspect of his life . . . his friends—if he had any—colleagues, hobbies, banking information, previous relationships, current relationships. Everything and everybody would be scrutinized. And they were trying to trace his Nigerian boy toy. She wondered how that line of enquiry was going. It flashed through her mind to ring Gareth to find out. She decided not to. It didn't seem right, somehow.

She took a sip of wine, put her feet up on the ottoman, settled back in her chair, and closed her eyes. Harrison jumped up in her lap and she stroked his soft fur, smiling as she listened to him purr. The sound of his purring grew louder. She blinked, and then started, when she realized through her twilight, drowsy haze that what she was hearing was not her purring cat but her ringing telephone.

"Hello?" she mumbled.

"Hello, Penny, is that you? Oh, I'm so sorry, I think I woke you up."

Penny recognized the soft Midwestern American accent. "No, no, Dorothy, I was just relaxing in my chair." A light laugh greeted this remark. "Now come on, Penny. I've roused Alan from a nap often enough to know what a sleepy voice sounds like." Dorothy Martin was a former American schoolteacher who, like Penny, had settled in Britain many years ago. She'd married the now-retired Chief Constable Alan Nesbitt, and the two travelled widely. She'd come to the Spa a few months ago and the two women had got to know each other over Dorothy's first manicure.

"Well, maybe I had drifted off," Penny admitted. "But I'm awake now and it's great to hear from you. How are you?"

"Very well, thank you, Penny. But here's the reason I'm calling. Alan and I are planning to visit some more Welsh castles in June and are hoping to see you and Gareth while we're in your neck of the woods. The dates aren't definite yet, and I know it's a long way off, but just wanted to let you know."

Penny hesitated. "I'd love to, but I can't speak for Gareth, so I can't say for sure. But perhaps closer to the time we'll be able to sort something out."

"Sure. Anyway, you can discuss it with him and let me know."

"He's rather busy just at the moment," Penny said. "You probably heard about the murders at Gladstone's Library."

"Oh, yes, but I only know what I read in the papers. I

understand there's been an arrest for the first one, but not the second, is that right?"

"That's exactly right. The police still don't know who did for poor old Shipton. Gareth doesn't think the two murders are connected, but I'm not so sure. There's usually something, some kind of link, however tenuous and far fetched it might seem."

"You know Alan always says that a murder victim has no secrets from the police. And once you uncover the big secret, the one he was most desperate to keep hidden, you usually uncover the motive. Which, of course, leads you to the killer."

"Now it's very interesting you should say that. I was thinking about secrets just before I dozed off. In this case, I'm wondering if someone was keeping a secret that's connected to a bigger secret. I'm wondering if other people in the organization were in on the secret, too."

"Could be." Dorothy was silent for a moment. "That's certainly not unheard of. Think of the dreadful business in the Catholic Church with all the child abuse. Officials very high up had to have known what was going on and they all kept the secret. They put the organization's reputation and interests ahead of the welfare of the children."

"And shame on them," said Penny.

"Exactly."

"Thanks for this, Dorothy. You've given me something to think about, as you usually do."

"Well, I do hope you and Gareth will be able to get together with us when we come to Wales. You haven't really mentioned him. Is everything all right there?"

"Oh, it's fine. I think we're just redefining how we want to be together."

Dorothy laughed. "Oh, is that what they call it now? Well, I'm sure it'll all work out the way it's meant to."

After a few more minutes of friendly chat, Dorothy wrapped up the call. "It was lovely speaking to you and we'll hope to see you in June. And please, do let me know how the investigation goes. I'm curious to know what poor old Shipton's secret turns out to be."

Penny mulled that over for a few minutes. Shipton's secret. Then she called a friend.

"Hello, Bronwyn. Wondering if I could take you to lunch. The Ivy. Tomorrow? Lovely. See you then."

Thirty-four

*T*he Ivy, named for the spectacular Virginia Creeper that covered every square inch of it, which attracted national media attention when it turned scarlet every autumn, was Penny's favourite eating place.

She had even been known to escape to the Ivy on a weekday afternoon, strolling across the town's historic three-arched bridge that spanned the River Conwy, pausing for a moment, resting her arms on the bridge's parapet, to admire the sparkling water that splashed through the valley as it flowed to the Irish Sea.

She hadn't seen Bronwyn since the warden had been arrested, but she had spoken to her on the telephone and apologized for the way things had ended. Bronwyn and Thomas had been gracious and grateful. And while they were sorry they'd been wrong about the warden's involvement in the death of Minty Russell, they were glad that the truth had come out.

"What do you fancy today?" she asked, as Bronwyn scanned the menu.

"Honestly, I don't know why I bother with this," Bronwyn said, closing the menu and placing it on the table. "I always look at it, then ignore it, and order the same thing."

"The Welsh rarebit?"

Bronwyn nodded. They gave their orders to the server and then Bronwyn raised an eyebrow and looked expectantly at Penny. "Well?" she said with a sly smile.

"All right. I'll get right to it. I'm hoping you can tell me more about poor old Shipton. What he was like. Your impression of him. You're very good at reading people, and I'd be very interested to know what you made of him."

Bronwyn laughed lightly. "Thomas and I were saying just last night we thought you'd be asking a few questions about him. In fact, we were surprised you didn't ask sooner."

She sat back in her chair and took a sip of water.

"Well, let me start with what Thomas says about him. The other rectors didn't care for him, for several reasons. He had a rather off-putting sense of arrogant entitlement . . . as if the rules didn't apply to him. The others had to submit reports, for example, but he couldn't be bothered. The bishop is fastidious about record keeping, and so he should be—parish records are important, and have been for centuries. They have to be accurate and they have to be up to date. But Shipton's were sloppy. The bishop was always threatening to send Minty over there to help him get caught up and make sure everything was shipshape." She grimaced at her little pun while Penny was taking in what she had just said.

So there was a connection between the two. Minty would have had complete access to Shipton's parish records. But still, as the bishop's secretary, that was to be expected. She smiled up at the server as she set their meals down in front of them.

"Will there be anything else for now?" she asked. Bronwyn shook her head and Penny told the server they were fine for the moment.

"Tell me about the parish records, Bronwyn, please."

Bronwyn cut off a piece of toast, piled some warm, gooey cheese on it, placed the fork in her mouth and closed her eyes. She chewed for a moment and swallowed.

"There are two types," she began. "There's the financial record. That's about accountability. The amount of revenue the parish raises, how it's spent. Or saved. Some money stays within the parish to cover operating costs and some is sent to the bishopric for the general good of the diocese."

"And the other?"

"This is the interesting one. This is a formal record of the births, marriages, and deaths within the parish. I suppose it would have legal standing, but I'm not sure. Anyway, the rectors are required to maintain legal records of these major life events. There's only one parish record book in use at one time, and sometimes it's retained at the church and sometimes it's held for safekeeping at the county record office. When the book is full, it's sent to the National Library of Wales, where it forms part of the national collection. Until about the mid-1800s, the church was the only keeper of this kind of information—*data,* people would call it now, I suppose. And then in the mid-1800s, civil records came into play so genealogists and amateurs who come here to Wales to trace their roots have two sources. But parish records are still important for historical record keeping."

"I see. And might anyone have access to the parish records? For example, if I wanted to view Thomas's records, could I do that? If I thought my great-aunt, say, had been married in the church, could I look that up myself?"

Bronwyn smiled. "Well, Thomas would let you look, I'm sure. He keeps his record in a locked cabinet in the vestry, in case you were wondering."

"I wasn't wondering about his, but I was wondering where Shipton kept his."

"I expect Thomas could find that out for you. Until a replacement can be found for Shipton, the bishop is sharing out his work amongst all the other parishes. In fact, Thomas is doing a wedding on Saturday that was originally scheduled to be performed by Shipton. You might want to come."

"Why would I want to see people I don't know get married?"

"I think it would interest you. An international couple. Thomas has concerns about the validity of the relationship."

"Really? Why?"

"Just come. Two o'clock. You'll see."

"Well, I'm intrigued. Will you be there?"

"Yes, Thomas has asked me to go. Apparently I'm to be a witness."

"A witness? You? Don't they have any friends? I thought the best man and bridesmaid were the witnesses."

"This is a little different than most weddings. Just turn up. You might be sorry if you don't."

"I'll do my best. Depends how many bookings we have. Saturday afternoons can be busy at the Spa." They ate for a few minutes in silence, and then Penny asked, "What parish did Shipton have? I don't think anyone told me that. Where was his church?"

"Oh, he had a very pretty church in Abergele. St. Michael's. Lovely old place."

"Is there anything more you can tell me about him, Bronwyn? I don't feel I've got the complete picture of him."

"Well, you know about his gentleman friend from Nigeria and how cross the bishop was about that. But no one cares these days that he was gay, although some church officials still take a dim view of it."

Bronwyn put her fork down.

"But the interesting thing is that he was married for over twenty years and had a couple of children. Daughters, I believe." She nodded. "Yes, it's true. He was from that generation when most gay men remained closeted. It may be they were in denial. And I think, sadly, there was a lot of shame associated with it." She shrugged. "Of course it wasn't talked about then. So many of these men married and had families. And then they went through a kind of midlife crisis, admitted to themselves that they were not living their authentic lives, told their families, and went on to establish relationships with gay partners. Of course, by the time all this happened, times had changed and society had become much more tolerant of homosexuality. More accepting, I should say." She sighed. "Thomas has done a bit of counseling on that issue."

"The men came to him for counseling, did they?"

"No, not the men. They were quite content once they were out and got on with their lives. It was the wives who were understandably devastated. How could I not have known, they asked themselves. Was there something I could have done differently? And of course they felt humiliated and embarrassed."

"So how long ago did this happen with Shipton? And where is his wife now, do you know?"

"It was, oh, two or three years ago. Judith, I think her name was. I don't know what happened to her. She used to be very active in the parish. Had a special interest in unwed mothers, as we used to call them. Single women having babies."

"Why did the bishop let Shipton keep his job?" Penny asked.

"There's a real shortage of rectors nowadays, Penny. Christianity numbers are dropping and very few young people are choosing to go into the church. Or go to church, for that matter. Practically everyone in our congregation is over fifty. No one has time for church anymore. In the old days, it used to be the centre of family life and everyone's social lives. Anyway, these days, a parish lucky enough to have a rector all to itself is very rare. Most rectors have to serve two or three parishes." She folded her hands in her lap.

"There's something I've been wanting to ask you, if you don't mind. When you discovered Shipton's body, what did he look like?"

"I've been thinking about that," replied Penny in a low voice and looking around to make sure no one could overhear. "I think it must have been especially awful for him.

He was twisted slightly in his chair as if he had heard someone approaching, then turned around to see who it was and saw the assailant coming toward him. He almost had a surprised look on his face."

"Well, he would be surprised, wouldn't he? No one gets up in the morning expecting to be murdered by lunchtime. I expect for most murder victims there's an element of surprise."

"Maybe. But I think he knew his attacker, and then a few terrible seconds later realized he was about to die."

Bronwyn shuddered. "That's too awful to think about. The poor man."

"I think I'm going to take an extra-long lunch today and hop on the bus to Abergele. I've a hankering to visit Shipton's church, and I'd also like to see if I could have a look at the parish records. Pretend I'm researching some family history. You know, I believe my great-aunt Henrietta came from these parts. There might be a caretaker or clerk or somebody about who could let me in."

"Penny, why would you want to do that? Why do you want to look at the records?" Bronwyn reached for her handbag and pulled out a tissue.

"It's just a hunch. I think Shipton was hiding a secret, and because he was so open about his personal life, I think it had to do with his work. It could be just a wild goose chase, though. Complete waste of time."

"Well, as a matter of fact, I might be able to save you some time. Thomas has brought over the parish records and they're locked away in our safe in the vestry that I told you about. He wanted to check if Shipton had made an entry for the wedding on Saturday already. You see, you have to record if the marriage is taking place by banns or licence and Shipton should have recorded that. Of course, he didn't. Thomas was annoyed, but not surprised. He'll have to ask the couple on Saturday if they have a licence, although he doubts the couple will understand the question."

"Why not?"

"Because neither of them speaks English."

"Oh." Penny thought for a moment. "Hmm. Seems there's more to getting married than you'd think. You mentioned banns or licence. What does that mean?"

"Calling the banns means the rector makes a public announcement of a forthcoming marriage, in the couple's parish church, for three Sundays in a row prior to the wedding and this gives an opportunity for anyone to object to the marriage—for example, because one of the parties was already married. Or a couple can get a licence if they don't want the banns read. Whatever the couple decides to do is recorded in the parish record."

"And Shipton should have recorded that."

"Yes."

"But he didn't?"

"No. Maybe he hadn't got around to it."

Penny thought about that for a moment and then set down her knife and fork.

"But will it make a difference if they arranged to get married in one parish—that is in Abergele—and now they're getting married in another—here in Llanelen?"

"It might, under normal circumstances but it probably won't matter in this case," Bronwyn said.

"Why not?"

"Because this wedding isn't going to take place," said Bronwyn with an enigmatic smile. "But that's enough. You'll see. Anyway, after we've finished lunch, let's go and talk to Thomas."

Half an hour later, they scrambled into their jackets, settled the bill, and left. While they had been having lunch, a light drizzle had begun to fall. The sky above them was dark, but across the valley a line of palest blue sky streaked across the hills bringing a promise of clear weather, and maybe even an early summer.

Bronwyn snapped open an umbrella and the women hurried across the bridge, past the Spa, and on to the rectory. "I expect he's in his study," said Bronwyn as she pushed open the door. "Have a seat," she said as they entered the warm kitchen. "I'll be right back. With him, I hope."

A few minutes later she reappeared with Rev. Thomas Evans right behind her and Robbie, her adored cairn terrier, trotting along in front, tail wagging. The little dog approached Penny, who was seated on a kitchen chair, and put his front paws on her knee. She bent down and scratched his tufty ears.

Reverend Evans smiled hello at Penny. "Bronwyn says you'd like to see the Register of Marriages from St. Michael's," he said, laying a large, green volume on the table. "I've found it makes pretty interesting reading myself."

Penny slowly lifted the front cover. "Turn to the most recent entries," said Reverend Evans. "Look at the names of the brides and grooms."

Each handwritten entry contained the date of the marriage, first and last names of the marrying couple, their marital status—in all cases, single—age, their addresses, the occupation of each, whether the marriage was taking place by banns or licence, and the name and occupation of the fathers of the bride and groom. Also included was the name of the person who performed the marriage.

"Look at the names," said Reverend Thomas, "and there are hundreds of them just like that."

Penny ran her finger down the pages. Women with first names like Ania, Rasa, Viktorija, Biata, Irina, Ludmilla, and Zusane were marrying men with first names like Azeem, Hussain, Wahee, Tariq, Abdi, and Akono.

"What is this?" Penny asked looking at Thomas while Bronwyn busied herself at the sink filling the kettle. "These people aren't Welsh. Or even British."

"They're no more Welsh than you are," said Thomas. "It could mean that Shipton was running a sham-marriage scam. He was taking in thousands of pounds performing sham marriages." He pointed to the names of one couple. "The woman, here, is Polish. She holds a European Economic Area passport. The man comes from Pakistan, I would say. More than likely, he's living in the UK illegally and wants the right to remain, to work and to collect benefits. A marriage broker, for a very large fee, probably put up by this man's family, arranged for him to marry this woman. She was probably paid about two thousand pounds to marry him. They will never live together in a genuine, committed relationship. And when all this blows over, enough time has passed, they will divorce and his family will arrange a marriage for him with some poor young woman from his native country. We've been asked to be on the lookout for this kind of thing."

"And Shipton would have known this?"

"Certainly he would have. He'd have known it over and over again."

"And Minty, would she have known about it?"

"She probably figured it out at some point. I expect Shipton recorded the marriages in the register, as required by law, and may have included some of them in his parish reporting, but he did not record the corresponding income from the marriages he performed. That would have gone straight in his pocket." He folded his arms. "The bishop was always on at Shipton about his sloppy and late record-keeping, and maybe now we know why. I heard that the bishop threatened a few to times to send Minty over to Abergele to sort Shipton out, but I don't know if she ever went."

"I need to think this through," said Penny, smiling her thanks briefly at Bronwyn, who placed a cup of tea in front of her. "I'm not sure it makes sense. You'd think that if he was up to something like this he would ensure his record keeping was immaculate. The last thing he'd want is the bishop complaining about his record keeping or Minty coming round to go through his books with a fine-toothed comb. But first things first. Have you informed Gareth about the wedding on Saturday? He'll know what to do."

"Yes, I have," replied Thomas. "He told me to say nothing to the couple. To just let them turn up thinking everything is all right and he'll take care of everything else."

"He and the UK Border Agency people," added Bronwyn. "They're coming to the wedding, too."

"But of course there isn't really going to be a wedding," said Thomas.

"I don't quite see what this means in terms of Shipton's death," said Penny, "although I'm sure that it's connected to it, in some way."

"At least we know Minty couldn't have done it," said Bronwyn. "She was already dead."

"Hmm," said Penny, preparing to close the record book. She lifted the heavy cover and let the large pages cascade closed. As they fluttered by a name caught her attention just before the page turned into the next one. "Oh!" she exclaimed. "What's that? I just saw a name I recognized."

"What name?" asked Bronwyn.

"Shipton," said Penny.

"Of course you saw his name. He performed all the marriages," said Thomas.

"No, it wasn't in that section. Wait. Let me find it. It was right here, about a third of the way down the page." She leafed slowly through the pages, until she came to the entry she was looking for.

"Look at this!" She checked the date. "Eight years ago. Bride: Rhosyn Grace Shipton. Groom: Hywel Leonard Stephens. Occupation: accountant." She looked from Thomas to Bronwyn. "Did you know that? Did you know that Hywel Stephens was married to Ros Shipton?"

"No," said Thomas. "I didn't know the family all that well. Or if I did know, I'd forgotten."

"Oh, the poor girl," said Bronwyn. "First she has to go through that business with her father, coming out as a gay man and leaving her mother, and then her husband setting up house and having another family with the Spanish woman." She glared at Thomas. "This is too much! It's enough to put you right off men."

She turned to Penny. "Now that you know all this, I'm sure you wouldn't miss the wedding on Saturday for the world. But don't waste one minute worrying about what to wear."

Thirty-five

*A*pparently the bride hadn't spent too much time worrying about what to wear, either. Danuta Jaworski's thin collarbone peeked out from an unflattering, creased, limp wedding dress in off white duchesse satin that had obviously been worn a few times without the benefit of dry cleaning between each wearing. The hem, which trailed on the ground, was rimmed with dirt. She had the pale, sallow face of a longtime smoker with heavy wrinkles around her lips, and her breath reeked of stale alcohol and cigarettes. Her age, as given on the marriage licence she produced, was thirty-six. She looked at least ten years older, as if she'd been ridden hard and put away wet. She had arrived at the church alone, nervous and unsmiling, clutching a cheap bunch of supermarket carnations. Thomas and Bronwyn had shown her into a small anteroom adjoining the rector's study, and gesturing to a chair, offered her something to drink and asked her to wait. Bronwyn had remained with her while Thomas returned to the main door of the rectory. A few minutes later Davies arrived. He extended his hand to Thomas and, after a whispered conversation, entered the rector's office and sat in one of the visitor's chairs. Next to arrive was Penny, and Thomas directed her to join Bronwyn and the Polish bride. When Sgt. Bethan Morgan, dressed in a plain black suit, slipped in through the Evans's kitchen door and joined them, Penny and Bronwyn gave her a relieved smile. The bride gave the three women a bored look, raised two slightly-separated fingers to her lips in a universal smoking gesture, handed her shabby bouquet to Bronwyn, and left the room.

Thomas rubbed his hands nervously together. As he stood on the stone step of the rectory, the wind gently lifted the green stole embroidered with a gold Celtic cross that he wore on top of his white surplice. A few moments later, Danuta emerged from the door behind him, walked onto the grass, and lit a cigarette. She inhaled deeply several times, blowing smoke out her mouth and nostrils, then dropped the cigarette and ground it into the dirt with a dirty gold strappy sandal. She brushed wordlessly past Thomas and returned to the anteroom.

As Thomas stood watch on the doorstep, a black car stopped in front of the river entranceway and two men got out of the back seat. The first, whom Thomas supposed to be the unfortunate bridegroom, had short, very black hair and wore a business suit with a bow tie. The second man who looked very much like the first, chattered away to his charge in a foreign language. Thomas surmised this was his translator. The front passenger door opened and a pair of highly polished black brogues emerged, belonging to a heavyset black man who showed very large white teeth set in a wide, easygoing smile as he caught sight of Rev. Thomas Evans.

"Good afternoon," said Thomas. "Right this way. If you would, please, go into my study. You will find a gentleman there waiting to speak to you." The translator said something, and the bridegroom looked around him uneasily. But the third man, who seemed to be in charge, said nothing, and confidently led the way down the hall in the direction Thomas had pointed. His expression changed when he entered the rector's study and saw Davies. He turned and tried to push his way past the bridegroom and best man behind him, but the short hallway that led to the open door through which he had just come was now filled with uniformed police and UK Border Agency officers, all wearing black tactical vests.

Seeing that he could not escape, the man stopped and turned around. Davies was waiting for him. "Azumi Odogwu, I am DCI Gareth Davies of the North Wales Police and I would like you to come in and sit down."

"Why? Who are you? What have I done? What do you want with me? I haven't done anything. You have no reason to keep me here."

Handing the bridegroom and his translator over to the nearest police officer, Davies closed the door and again told Odogwu to sit down. The man sank slowly into a chair in front of the desk and refused to make eye contact with either

Davies or Constable Chris Jones, who stood nearby with his back against the wall.

"Now then. First, I want to confirm that you are in fact Azumi Odogwu. Is that your name?"

The man said nothing.

"Very well," said Davies. "We'll come back to that. Let's move on. Did you arrange the marriage that was to take place here today?"

"No, no! It was nothing to do with me."

"Well, we'll all be going down to the police station in a few minutes to sort everything out," said Davies, "but I should warn you those people out in the corridor there," he said, gesturing at the door, "are with the UK Border Agency and they're going to start by taking a very close look at your passport. If your passport proves to be a forgery, you will be charged with possession of a false passport. And if our investigation shows that you have been involved in arranging sham marriages, you will be charged with conspiracy to assist unlawful immigration."

"No, no," Odogwu repeated, "I haven't done anything. I live here simply and quietly."

"Do you, Mr. Odogwu? Do you really? Where do you live?"

Odogwu did not reply. "Abergele, isn't it, Mr. Odogwu? You were a good friend of Nigel Shipton, I believe?"

"I don't know any Shipton," he said.

"Well, that's strange, because I have at least twenty witnesses, including a bishop, who can testify that you recently attended a party with Mr. Shipton at Gladstone's Library. And at that party he introduced you as his friend, Azumi Odogwu." Davies made a display of consulting his notes.

Odogwu's dark brown eyes widened. "Look, Mr. Odogwu," said Davies, "you could be in a lot of trouble here. You're looking at several years in prison if you have broken British immigration laws." Odogwu struggled to get to his feet but Jones placed a restraining hand on his shoulder. "But the UK Border Agency will take care of all that. There's something else, another matter, that you and I have to talk about Mr. Odogwu. Do you know what that is?" Odogwu shook his head.

"We need to talk about the murder of the Reverend Nigel Shipton. What can you tell me about that?" Odogwu did not reply. "Right," said Davies with a nod at Jones. "Mr. Odogwu might be more forthcoming at the station. Constable Jones, please arrest him and we'll bring him in for an interview."

In the small anteroom where Penny and Bronwyn sat with the bride, as the time for the wedding came and went, the tension became unbearable. The woman sat with one leg over the other, jiggling her foot up and down. As the annoyance factor increased, Penny glanced at Bronwyn, who gave a worried shrug. Both turned to Sgt. Bethan Morgan, who gave a noncommittal shake of her head. The bride looked at her watch, coughed, and stood up. She said something in a language no one understood. Bethan motioned for her to sit down and the waiting resumed. A few minutes later, when Penny thought she couldn't take one more second of the irritating foot jiggling, the door opened and Gareth Davies stuck his head in. If he was surprised to see Penny, he did not show it.

He made eye contact with Bethan, then tipped his head at the bride. "We're ready for her now," he said. Bethan tapped the woman on the shoulder, made a small "get up" gesture with her hand, and then ushered her from the room. Davies came in and closed the door.

"Thank you, Bronwyn," he said, and then turned to Penny. "I didn't expect to see you here."

"No, I'm sure you didn't," she replied. "Bronwyn asked me to come along today, so here I am." Davies looked puzzled but said nothing.

"What will happen to the bride?" Bronwyn asked.

"The Border people will look into her history," said Davies, "and try to determine if she is who her passport says she is and, depending on what they turn up, she may or may not be charged. She was probably paid a couple of thousand pounds to marry that guy. So sad and pathetic that women are willing to go with through with a sham marriage for what doesn't amount to a whole lot of money. I expect it gets used up pretty quickly and then she's saddled with a man she doesn't even know."

"And what about the bridegroom?" Penny asked.

"He paid someone a huge amount of money, probably upwards of ten thousand pounds, to arrange this marriage for him," Davies said. "We want to find out if that someone was Mr. Odogwu. And then we'll want to know if Mr. Odogwu is the orchestra leader or if he's just the page-turner for somebody else."

"Do you think he had anything to do with the murder of Shipton?" Penny asked.

"He may be connected to it in some way, but I don't know yet how deep his involvement was. But let's hope he'll be able to tell us something."

PC Chris Jones stuck his head in the door, acknowledged Bronwyn and Penny, and then spoke to Davies.

"We're leaving now, sir. We'll see you at the station." Before he left, Davies gave Penny an odd look that she could not read. She felt an uneasiness and turned to Bronwyn, who returned her unspoken concern.

"I wonder what they'll get out of Odogwu," Bronwyn said.

"It's about the money," Penny said in a low voice. "It's got to be about the money."

"But why would they kill Shipton?" Bronwyn asked. "Wouldn't that be like killing the goose that laid the golden eggs? He performed the marriages for them. Without him, everything fell apart and that's the end of the money."

Penny nodded and looked thoughtful. "I wonder." She straightened up and prepared to leave. "Anyway, I hope they get some useful information out of Odogwu."

"I bet he sings like a canary," said Bronwyn grimly. "He looks the type."

"Sings like a canary?" Penny laughed in spite of herself. "Have you been staying up late again watching old Humphrey Bogart movies?"

Thirty-six

*D*o you want to have lunch?"

Victoria had popped into Penny's manicure room just as Penny was tidying up after the morning's appointments. She gathered up two or three white towels and tossed them into a laundry basket, then set the used tools aside ready to be packaged for the sterilizer.

"Oh, thanks, Victoria, but not today. I've got an errand to run. There's someone I want to see." Penny picked up a bottle of nail varnish remover and a small glass bottle of cotton balls.

"Where are you going with those?" Victoria asked.

"I'm going to make a house call."

"We make house calls now?'

"Not really. But this is a special case."

"Is Mrs. Lloyd ill and unable to make her appointment this afternoon?"

"No, it's not that. I want to check up on Ros Stephens. It's been over a week since she was in here for her manicure and I doubt she's been out of the house since. If she doesn't have any nail varnish remover in, her nails will be chipped by now and looking really dreadful. I always think that look is so demoralizing. Can't stand it."

"But Penny, it's not up to you to follow our clients around and go to their homes to make sure their manicures are looking good."

"I know it isn't, but she's been through a terrible time. That awful business with her husband and the loss of her father."

"Her father died?"

"Didn't you know? No, of course you didn't. I didn't have a chance to tell you. Ros's father was Nigel Shipton."

Victoria looked puzzled.

"The Reverend Nigel Shipton. The body in Gladstone's Library."

"Oh, I see." She considered this for a moment. "I did not know that. Still, Shipton wasn't from around here, so I doubt many people will know he was her father."

"Well," said Penny settling her bag over her shoulder, "I'll see you later."

The day was clear and warm, with soft clouds swirling playfully around the hilltops in a sky of unusually bright azure blue. It was a day to be outdoors, with a pair of comfortable walking boots on your feet, a light jacket on your back, and all the time you needed to enjoy wherever you were going.

Penny walked along the river, past a renovation building project that was seeing an empty warehouse turned into expensive flats with river views and turned up Rosemary Lane, a small street of solid, detached houses. The house at the end of the street was slightly larger than the others. As she approached the front door she took in the closed curtains. She looked for a doorbell, and not seeing one, lifted the metal flap that covered the letter slot and banged it two or three times. A moment later a disembodied voice called from inside the house. "Who is it?"

Penny bent over and spoke through the letter slot.

"Ros, it's me, Penny Brannigan from the Llanelen Spa."

A moment later the door was opened, cautiously and slowly.

"Oh, Penny, come in. I was afraid you might be a reporter. I've had a couple of phone calls. I don't want to talk to them."

Penny stepped into the small entryway and bent to take off her shoes. "No, leave them," said Ros. "I haven't been about to bring myself to get out the Hoover since . . . well, never mind." She gestured toward the sitting room. "Come through."

"I expect you're surprised to see me," said Penny, "and I do apologize. I should have rung you first." She reached out to Ros and with a "May I" look, loosely picked up her hand and examined her fingernails. The gleaming, carefully applied coral varnish was now chipped. A sliver of pink nail at the top of the nail showed where the nail had grown and the polish at the tip was jagged and unsightly. "I was afraid of this," said Penny. "It doesn't do good things for your state of mind when your nails look like this.

I brought the remover. Would you let me take this off for you? You're much better off with no polish than this."

Ros looked at her nails in a curious way as if seeing them for the very first time. "I hadn't even thought about them but you're right. They do look awful."

Her mouth trembled as she sank into the sofa. "You came over here to do this for me?" she asked. "Why would you do that?"

"Because I want to do this one very small thing in case it helps you feel better." Penny dabbed some remover onto a cotton ball and began swiping at Ros's thumb nail.

"And because I want to talk to you."

"Oh, please, don't ask me anything about him."

"No, it's not him, Ros. It's your father, Nigel Shipton. You see, I was there. In fact, I was the one who found his body."

Thirty-seven

"You found his body? You were at the Library?"

"Yes, I was. I did. And I wanted to come and see you in case you have any questions. And speaking of questions, have the police been to see you yet, by the way?"

Ros shook her head.

"No, well, you might want to prepare yourself for a visit," said Penny.

"Not too many people know that we're related," said Ros. "How did you find out, by the way?"

"I had an opportunity to go through the Register of Marriages from your father's church in Abergele," said Penny. "And I spotted your name. I thought it was rather charming that your father married you. That must have been a lovely moment."

"Well, yes and no," said Ros. "My father couldn't stand

Hywel. Oh, he respected him professionally, but didn't like him personally. Daddy thought there was something dangerous about him. He wasn't keen on my marrying him; he thought I was letting myself in for more than I bargained for." She gave a sad little snort of belated understanding. "And as it turned out, he was right."

She reached up to refasten her honey brown hair with the large clip that held it on top of her head and then peered at Penny. "You heard all about Hywel and the Spanish woman?"

Penny nodded.

"Yes," said Ros. "Of course you did. Everyone's heard about it. That's why I haven't been out of the house in days. I can't bear to have anyone look at me with their terrible pity." She looked at her fingernails, now free of the chipped polish. "It was really good of you to stop by to sort out my nails. When Daddy left us, my mother didn't want to go out of the house, either. She moved away. She's been very supportive of me in all this. She understands exactly what I'm going through."

And then, after a moment's silence, Ros asked, "Would you like a cup of tea?"

"I'd love one."

Ros got up and a few minutes later the sound of running water in the kitchen filtered into the sitting room as Ros filled the kettle. Then came the comforting domestic rattle of cups, saucers, and spoons being set out on a tray. Penny looked around the room, taking in all the photos of a small boy. If there had been family photos that included the boy's father, they had been removed.

"I didn't know what to think when Mum told me

Daddy had been murdered," Ros said when she returned. "We had been estranged for the past few years, Daddy and I, after he put his midlife crisis before all of us. My mother and sister and me. But lately I'd been thinking about my son, Tudur. That's him, there," she said, her voice shaded with pride as she pointed to the photos on the mantelpiece. "I thought about him growing up not knowing his grand-dad and was that fair to him. Grandparents can bring such joy into a child's life. So I was just starting to wonder if there would be a way to have Daddy in Tudur's life with-out upsetting my mother, when all this happened."

"It must have been terribly difficult going through the death of your father and the business with your husband at the same time," Penny said. "I cannot imagine what that must have been like."

Ros gave a little shrug and then a heartbreaking little laugh. "Well, of course it's over between Hywel and me. An affair is one thing, but to set up home and have a child with someone is the ultimate betrayal. I'll never get past that." She looked thoughtful. "And yet, in all this, I have to keep reminding myself that it is not that child's fault. That child had nothing to do with this. And that child is actually my Tudur's half-brother. So the big loser in all this mess is Tudur. He's lost a grandfather he barely knew, a half-brother he never knew, and his father, whom he adores."

When the kettle whistled, Ros stood up. "Listen to me going on. But you can't imagine what a relief it is to put into words all these thoughts that have been going through my head. You'd be surprised how people keep away from you at a time like this."

"They may not know what to say," said Penny. "They

may be afraid of asking too many questions or saying the wrong thing."

"Maybe," said Ros. "I'll be right back."

She returned a few minutes later and set a tray down on the coffee table. "Help yourself," she said. "The milk's good. My friend next door, who's been looking after Tudur while I fall apart, has been great about getting in things for me."

"Oh, right," said Penny. "Sorry, I didn't think. I should have asked if you needed anything."

"I don't need anything brought in, but I need some stuff taken away," Ros said. "I'll get it when you leave. It's in a bag upstairs."

"Fine," said Penny. "Not a problem. Whatever I can do."

She took a sip of tea and then set down her cup.

"There is something I wanted to ask you, and if you don't want to talk about it, just say so."

"Is it about my father?"

Penny nodded. "Fine," said Ros. "And then I want to ask you a question or two of my own about him."

"Well," said Penny. "It's like this. Murders generally don't just happen out of the blue. Oh, sometimes there are those awful situations you hear about on the news when a deranged or mentally ill person pushes a stranger to their death on the underground, but normally, murders don't happen that way. Usually, there's a situation that develops, often over time, but sometimes quite quickly and the murderer feels pushed to act."

Ros nodded.

"I was hoping you could tell me a little bit about your father so I could get to know him better. Get a sense of who he was as a person."

"You feel a connection to him because you found him, is that it?"

"Yes, you could say that."

"Right. Well, growing up I didn't have any sense of what my parents' marriage was like, or what the truth of it was, but children shouldn't be part of that. The relationship should be private between the two grown-ups. They say it's not a good thing to fight in front of your children, and my parents didn't. Whatever was going on, they kept it behind closed doors and that's the way it should be.

"So it came as a huge shock when my mother told me and my sister that Daddy had told her he was a homosexual and was leaving her to get in touch with his gay side, or however he put it.

"And then off he went on holiday somewhere and came back with that odious man, Odogwu, as his companion. My poor mother was so humiliated; she didn't want to show her face in the town. Everyone was talking about us; it was the juciest scandal to hit Abergele in some time, I can tell you."

"Yes, I bet it was," agreed Penny. "But things do blow over and people forget and move on."

Ros nodded. "Still, my mother didn't want to stay, so she moved away. I was married and living here in Llanelen with Hywel. We were happy, or at least I thought we were.

"But what struck me about poor Daddy and his midlife crisis was that something had gone terribly wrong with him. It seemed as if his filters had been switched off and all his inhibitions were gone. I thought Odogwu was taking advantage of him. Using him for his own ends, like."

"You may be right, Ros."

"There was just something about Daddy's wild behaviour that was so out of keeping with his character. He used to be very conservative and staid, and then suddenly to be wearing brightly coloured shirts and loud, clunky jewellery just didn't seem like him.

"And the money! Apparently he was spending money wildly on all sorts of things he didn't need or even want. He bought some kind of rare, purebred dog that cost thousands of pounds and then a few weeks later gave it away to a couple of kids he met at a homeless youth shelter. I felt terrible when my sister told me about that. For the dog, not the money."

"And your sister," said Penny. "Where is she?"

"Oh, she's with my mother in Manchester. They were always close, those two, and . . ." Her voice trailed off.

"You were close to your dad," finished Penny for her.

Ros's eyes glistened with unshed tears and she nodded. "Yes," she said softly. "And when he died, at first I was conflicted but then it was as if all that lost time fell away and none of it mattered anymore."

"What about funeral arrangements?" Penny asked.

"I don't know," Ros said. "I doubt my mother will claim his body."

"And if the police or authorities don't know about you, as his daughter, then they can't get in touch," said Penny. "Should you think about doing that for your father? So that if the manner of his death wasn't dignified and respectful, at least you would have the comfort of knowing that you did everything you could for him after that."

Ros nodded slowly, and the tiniest flash of relief and

brightness flashed across her face. "I didn't look at it that way, but you may be right. I'll think about it."

"I can give you the name of a police officer to call. He'll know what to do," said Penny. "But maybe don't mention we had this little chat when you speak to him."

"Right." Ros stood up. "I can't tell you how much better I feel. It was a huge relief to get those things out. I can't talk about my father with my mother and I can't talk about Hywel with my friends, who just want to bash him." She glanced at her watch. "Sorry, I have to pick up Tudur. He has a play date next door. My neighbour's been wonderful looking after Tudur, but I don't want to abuse her kindness. I'm just trying to keep everything as normal as I can for him."

"Yes, that's best, I'm sure," said Penny, "although I know next to nothing about children. Still, it seems sensible."

"Let me get that bag of Hywel's things. I haven't started packing up his clothes yet. He may want to come and get them, I don't know. I'm just getting rid of the small stuff for now."

"This may be very cold comfort," said Penny, "but I doubt very much if the relationship with the Spanish woman will survive this. It was fine as long as no one knew and he probably found it all hugely exciting but now that it's out in the open," she shook her head, "I would be very surprised if it lasts. So in the end, he'll lose everything he loved and that mattered to him."

Ros managed a weak smile. "So did I," she said, "but there's a certain justice in it if he does lose everything. If it happens. I thought the same thing myself."

She disappeared upstairs and returned a few minutes

later with two plastic carrier bags. "Here you go," she said, handing them to Penny. "If you don't mind dropping them at the charity shop."

"I wonder," said Penny. "This time of year Bronwyn's always so desperate for good items for her church jumble sale. Would it be all right if we put them in her sale rather than letting the charity shop have them?"

"It doesn't matter to me what you do with them, Penny, as long as they go to a good cause and they're out of the house and I don't have to look at them anymore. There's some good stuff in that lot."

As Penny turned to go, Ros let out a little shriek. "Hang on just a moment, Penny. There's something else." She dashed into the kitchen, returned with a plastic bag and bolted to the bookcase. She pulled out a few volumes and dropped them in the bag.

"Here," she said, holding out the bag to Penny. "Can you manage these as well? The other bags aren't too heavy and if you could get rid of these books, that would be great."

Penny peered in the bag. "Sure."

"They're Harry Potters. Hywel loved Harry Potter. Read all of them."

"But don't you want to keep them for your son?" Penny asked. "He'll be ready for them in a couple of years, won't he?"

"When he is, I'll buy him his own books. Those ones," she gestured at the carrier bag, "those ones I don't want anymore."

"All right," said Penny. "Leave it with me. I'll see that all of this gets sorted."

"That would be great, Penny. I do feel better. Thanks

for taking care of those bags. And for listening." She closed the door behind Penny, after catching a glimpse of the twitching net curtain at the attractive stone house across the way on Rosemary Lane, where Mrs. Lloyd and Florence Semble lived, and returned to the sitting room. She sat down on the beige sofa and looked at the name and number of the police officer Penny had given her.

I'll call him when I get home from picking up Tudur, she thought, setting the paper down beside the telephone and reaching for her house keys.

Thirty-eight

O h, hello, Penny," said Bronwyn into the telephone as she shifted a few items around in her refrigerator. "No, this is a perfectly good time. I was just thinking about what to have for dinner."

"I've got some items for your jumble sale," said Penny. "I haven't been through them yet, but I expect they're pretty nice. Used to belong to Hywel Stephens."

"Used to?"

"His wife bundled them all up and gave them to me to take to the charity shop, but I asked if I could give them to you instead for the jumble sale."

Bronwyn closed the refrigerator door.

"Penny, in that case then, I am not sure they are hers to give. If they belong to Hywel Stephens, then I believe it is he who makes the donation, not an angry, scorned wife, no matter how good her intentions. Hell hath no fury, re-member. And we would not want to be liable if he turned up demanding his property and we had to say, oh, sorry, we sold it in the spring jumble sale."

Penny gasped and placed her hand over her mouth. "Oh, gosh. I never thought of that. Yikes."

"At least, I think that's our position. This same situation happened once before and that's what Thomas told me. If Thomas says we can't take it, you could always give it to the charity shop I suppose, but I'd be careful if I were you, because you're the one who is actually getting rid of his property, if you see what I mean. And it isn't really yours to give away."

"You're absolutely right. Well, I'll just hang on to it. He may turn up looking for it as he's got to come back sooner or later and he might want it then. The main thing for now is that it's out of the house and Ros doesn't have to look at it. I think that's what mattered most to her."

"I suppose it was awfully good stuff," said Bronwyn wistfully. "Mr. Stephens always looked very well-turned out. I suppose there are nice ties and such."

"I didn't really look at it," said Penny. "Just peeked in the bag, the way you do. There were some ties and small boxes. The ties looked to be of very good quality, I must say, although I don't know that much about them. But I did spot a very nice designer label or two." There was a silence at the end of the line.

"Still, I'd be curious to know what I've passed up," said Bronwyn finally.

"Well, shall I come over?" asked Penny. "This is definitely something we don't want to be doing at the Ivy over a Welsh rarebit."

"No, we don't," agreed Bronwyn. "And maybe we've had enough Welsh rarebit for the time being."

"Delicious though it is."

"I think it might be better if I came to you," said Bronwyn. "So you don't have to be carrying it around and Thomas doesn't see us. The evenings are staying lighter much later now, so how about I walk Robbie over to yours after supper? If you were to have coffee and cake on offer, I wouldn't say no."

"Cake from the Ivy?"

"Mm. Chocolate or carrot, if possible."

"Sounds great. See you about seven?"

Penny spooned some coffee into the French press, filled it with hot water, and set it aside. She cut each piece of cake into two and set the two halves on plates. "I thought we'd have a sliver of carrot and walnut cake each," Penny said, handing a plate to Bronwyn.

"Oh, lovely. Aren't we are lucky to live so close to such a wonderful bakery?" Bronwyn raised a fork. "Shall we eat first and then go through the bags?"

"Yes," agreed Penny. "Why don't we? We don't want to touch anything with sticky fingers or spill coffee."

A few minutes later Bronwyn put down her fork. "That was a lovely treat, but I couldn't manage something like that every day. I'll just leave my coffee here," she said, setting her cup on the kitchen counter, "and let's see what there is. What do you say we tip everything out on the table and sort it into piles?"

"Sounds good to me," said Penny, upending the first bag. A jumble of ties, jewellery, and fragrance boxes tumbled onto the table.

"Let's see what we have," said Bronwyn, examining the label on a tie. "Hermès." She set it down and picked up a box of cologne. "I don't think this has even been opened. Ralph Lauren."

Penny picked up a black box and looked inside. It contained two watches, a man's and a woman's. "Emporio Armani. My, my."

She opened another box.

"This might be the watch he was wearing at the conference," she said. "I noticed something like this on him. I remember the wings. Thought it looked very smart." She weighed it in her hand. "Feels heavy."

"I always thought Hywel Stephens had very nice taste, if only a little obvious. You'd see him in the town, in his smart suit, looking so well dressed. I wonder where he bought these things. Nobody around here sells them. We don't even have a shoe store in Llanelen any more," said Bronwyn.

"He might order them online. Or go to Manchester to get them."

And then it hit both of them at the same time.

"He shops in airports. All this is duty-free swag," said Bronwyn, gesturing at the boxes.

"If it's genuine. Could be knockoffs." They looked at each other.

"Does he seem like the knockoff type to you?" Bronwyn half closed her eyes and shook her head. "I don't think so either. He seems like a nothing-but-the-best kind of man."

"So the next question is," said Penny, "how did he pay for all this? And keep up a household in Spain?"

She handed Bronwyn the second bag. "Here, you take a look through that. I'll be back in a minute."

"Where are you going?"

But the only reply was the sound of light footsteps running up the stairs. Penny returned a few minutes later with her laptop. "Let's have a look at that watch with the wings," she said. "I've heard of Rolex watches, of course, but not this one. She typed in the name on the watch, waited a few minutes, browsed a few pages and then let out a little yelp.

"What is it?" asked Bronwyn.

"This watch," said Penny, "if it's real, it's is worth about six thousand pounds. It's a Breitling."

"Oh, my Lord," exclaimed Bronwyn. "That would practically buy us a new roof! What on earth was his wife thinking, trying to donate all this to the charity shop?"

"That's just it," said Penny. "She isn't thinking, so we have to think for her. It could be that all these items will have to be appraised and their value listed as joint assets and taken into account for the divorce settlement." Bronwyn raised an eyebrow. "Oh, yes, Bronwyn, you must see that a divorce is inevitable. No amount of forgiveness or counseling will get them past what he's done. Having a child with another woman is a dealbreaker."

"I suppose it is."

"Anyway, what do you think we should do now? I'm so glad you realized that we didn't have the right to dispose of all this."

"I think we'd better ring Gareth."

"Yes, he'll know what to do for the best." Bronwyn glanced at the clock in the kitchen and then let out a little squeak. "Goodness, is that the time? I'd best be off. There's a program on telly tonight that Thomas and I are looking forward to. About water. How water is going to become the Earth's most precious resource. Prince Charles is doing the introduction."

Thirty-nine

So you're back." Victoria folded her hands together and set them on her desk. Her mouth was set in a tight line and her shoulders were squared and lifted.

"Yes, I'm back," said Penny. "I am sorry I've been away so much. I'll do better going forward, I promise. Oh, and here's the signed contract for the Dilys hand cream." She set the brown envelope on table and slid it toward Victoria.

"Well, actually, Penny, there's something I need to talk to you about," she said as she picked up the envelope.

"Oh, yes?" Penny picked up her handbag and began poking about inside. Victoria waited. As the silence deepened, Penny stopped what she was doing and looked up.

"What? What is it?"

"I've thought about the best way to tell you this and I don't think there's an easy way." Penny's eyes widened as a twist of fear and anxiety shot through her. "You're not," she said, "don't tell me you're leaving."

"I'm sorry, Penny, I'm very sorry. But you remember that man I met on holiday in Italy . . ."

Penny groaned. "Victoria, he's married. Don't do something you'll regret."

"We've been e-mailing and talking on the phone. He's left his wife. He's moved out and he wants me to come and stay with him, and I'm going to."

"So what does this mean for our business?" Penny asked in a low, cold tone. "If you want to make a fool of yourself with some Italian, while I'd hate to see you get hurt, that's your choice. But what are you planning to do about the business?"

"Oh, Penny, please, no, it's only for a bit. I'm so sorry. I realize it must have sounded as if I'm going for good. I'm not. I thought maybe six weeks or so. I've been training up Rhian and thought we could put her in as manager and maybe hire a temp to take over the reception duties."

She picked up a paperclip and began opening and twisting it. She toyed with it for a few moments and then set it down on the desk

Victoria smiled. "I know you're not happy with what I'm doing and the implications for the business, but please, Penny, do try to be happy for me. If I don't go, I'll always wonder."

"You've given me a lot to think about. Let's leave it at that for now."

But as Penny left the room, it wasn't what Victoria had said that bothered her. It was something she'd seen.

She returned to the manicure room where Eirlys, her

young assistant, was busy with a client. She looked up as Penny entered.

"You all right for the rest of the afternoon, Eirlys?"

"Yes, Penny, thanks, I am."

"Good. I've got to go and see someone, but if something comes up I've got my mobile so if you need me, just ring."

On the way out she let Rhian know she was leaving and then, as the implications of what Victoria had just told her jostled for head room with a glimmer of an idea about the murder of Nigel Shipton, she hurried home.

Forty

"Can I see you?" Penny wrapped the telephone cord around her finger.

"Of course you can see me," Davies replied. "When?"

"As soon as possible," Penny replied.

"I'm just on my way into a briefing, but I'll try to get away by four. Should be with you by five. Is that soon enough?"

"It'll have to be, I guess," Penny smiled into the telephone.

"Do you want me to bring anything?" Penny thought he was hinting at dinner or a bottle of wine, but she ignored that.

"Yes, there is something I'd like you to bring, if you don't mind. The Shipton crime-scene photographs."

Davies groaned. "Aw, Penny, please. You know I can't do that. Is that what this is about?"

"Yes. I may be able to help you. I think I know something. And you don't even have to bring all the photos. I just want to see what was on the table where Shipton was working, so if there's one taken after the body was removed just showing the desk, that's the one I need. As long as nothing's been touched."

"I'll have a word with Bethan and see what I can do."

"Thanks, Gareth. Do it just this once and you won't be sorry. At least, I hope not."

A few minutes after five he arrived at Penny's cottage accompanied by his sergeant, Bethan Morgan. "Thought we'd be best keep the visit official," he said, gesturing at Bethan as they entered the sitting room.

"Of course," said Penny, following him to the sofa. Bethan opened an official-looking brown envelope, pulled out an eight-by-ten photo and handed it to Penny.

"Here's the photo of the desk taken just after the body was removed," she said.

Penny examined it for the briefest of moments. "I thought so," she said, nodding slowly. "I noticed it at the time, but it didn't register with me. But now, I think Shipton was trying to tell us something." She handed the photo to Davies. "Do you see it?"

He examined the photo. "It's the table in the Library Shipton was working at. Here are his glasses, the books he was reading or working from, a couple of pens, a few paperclips, some loose leaf pages. . . ." He looked at Penny. I don't see anything unusual here. What am I supposed to be looking at?"

"The paperclips. See how these two over here are normal, but this one," she pointed to one in the centre of the
table, "has been opened. It looks like either the number 5
or the letter S."

"So it does," said Davies, "but I don't see . . ."

He held out his hand out to Bethan. "Give me the
photo with Shipton still at the table." She selected the one
he wanted and passed it to him. He examined the photo
and then nodded slowly. "Yes, now I see." He placed the
photo on the coffee table and turning the first photo over
so it was white side up, covered part of the second photo.
He invited Penny to have a look. "Here's Shipton's hand
and a bit of his arm," he said. "I've covered up the body;
you don't have to look at it. But you can clearly see that the
index finger of his right hand is pointing at the paperclip."
He looked from one to the other. "Coincidence, or is he
trying to tell us something?"

"Let's assume he's trying to tell us something. If it's the
letter S, what could that mean?" asked Bethan.

"I think it points to Hywel Stephens," said Penny.

"Why?" asked Davies.

"Because he needed money to support his complicated
family life. He had two families in two countries. Shipton
was officiating at the sham weddings, pocketing the fees
himself, and not reporting the income. But, to keep the
fraud going he would have had to pay Stephens to fiddle
the books. Otherwise, the bishop would have found out
that money was missing."

Davies nodded slowly. "And then Miss Russell noticed the discrepancy in the high number of marriages in
Shipton's parish, but the parish wasn't bringing in the

corresponding income. There should have been more money."

He put the photo back in the envelope. "The bishop told me that Miss Russell had tried to speak to him the night of the opening reception, and she was waving about some kind of spreadsheet, but that he had brushed her off. I wonder if that's what she wanted to speak to him about? I wonder where that paper is now. We didn't turn up anything like that when we went through her things."

He thought for a moment.

"And then when the bishop refused to speak to her, she thought, right, we'll see about that and then hatched her little blackmail scheme."

He turned to Bethan. "Check with the tech team to see what they've come up with on Minty Russell's computer. Especially the deleted items. Tell them we're looking for a spreadsheet or a chart . . . something with numbers on it." He smiled at Penny. "We always find the deleted items much more interesting."

Bethan rubbed her eyes and stifled a yawn. "I'm sorry, Bethan," Penny said. "I should have asked. Could I get you a tea? Coffee?"

"I'd love a tea, thanks, Penny. Let me make it." She raised an eyebrow at Davies. "Sir?"

"Yes, I think I would," replied Davies.

"I'll make a pot, then. Won't be long."

With Bethan out of the room, Penny realized why Davies had brought her. The silence between them was heavy and awkward. "So," Davies said, finally, "have you been out sketching much?"

"I've been too busy in the Spa," Penny said. "We've got

268

some big changes coming there." She filled him in on Victoria's situation. "You'll miss her," said Davies. "In all kinds of ways."

"Yes, but she's gone away before and we were just fine. We'll miss her but we'll manage, as an old boss of mine used to say."

Bethan returned with a tray and set it down on the table. When she had poured tea for everyone, Davies took a sip, put his cup down, sat back, and closed his eyes. He folded his hands together in a praying gesture and held them in front of his lips. "Now then, let's revisit Shipton's death. Bethan, can you read us the statements of where people were at the time of the murder, please."

Bethan flipped open her notebook and turned a few pages.

"Here we are. The murder is estimated to have taken place about 1:10 P.M., give or take a few minutes either way."

"And of course those few minutes are critical to the timing," Davies interjected. "Let's see if we can place Stephens." He nodded at Bethan to continue.

"Mrs. Lloyd and Florence Semble were waiting in the Gladstone Room for Penny, as the three of them were to share a taxi to Chester railway station. Florence was reading the newspaper. She then went out in the hall to look for Penny. She had a clear view all the way to the Library. If Stephens had been in the hall, she would have seen him. She didn't see anyone."

"And Mrs. Lloyd?"

"I don't have a note here about her. I interviewed them together and they said they were together in the Library."

"And Stephens?"

"He said he left as soon as he could. He had no further business there, and had appointments scheduled with clients in Llanelen. He said he'd already stayed longer than he wanted to and was anxious to get away."

"So what time did he leave?"

"He said he left just after the hearse went by. He said he walked with the Blaines to the car park, said good-bye to them there, and they got in their respective cars and drove away."

"Did you confirm that with the bishop?"

"No, but I will."

"Ring him now." Davies and Penny listened as Bethan went through a series of yeses, I sees, and then thanked the bishop.

"Bishop Blaine confirms that they met Stephens in the parking lot, but says that he and his wife left first so he can't be absolutely certain that Stephens did in fact leave at the same time although he did see him getting into his car."

"So he could have gone back into the building," Penny said.

"He could have. But we haven't been able to find anyone who saw him at the scene. If we're going to consider him a suspect, we need to establish he was at the scene and had the opportunity. Or, to put it another way, to eliminate him from our enquiries, we need to establish that he was someplace else." He checked his watch. "It's almost five thirty. I hope his assistant is still at the office. Bethan, ring her and see if he kept those appointments he mentioned."

Bethan excused herself and went into the kitchen.

"He returned to the office about four o'clock, went to his computer, printed out some documents, and left," she said when she returned a few minutes later. "He had called her earlier and asked her to reschedule all his appointments for that day. And the next day, he left for Spain."

"What time did he call her?"

"She couldn't remember exactly. But the first appointment was at two, and she managed to ring that client in time to let him know the appointment was being rescheduled and not to come in."

Bethan looked at Davies and nodded. "Right. I'll start work on the timeline. We need to account for his every minute."

When the two police officers had gone, Penny sat with Harrison on her lap, thinking. It was all such a jumble of who was where and who said what to whom and who saw who with whom. She'd leave all that to the police to figure out. She had better things to worry about, and worried she was.

After a few minutes she gathered up the tea things and carried them through to the kitchen. It was too early to think about supper. What she really felt like was a walk. A few months ago she had been looking after Trixxi, the dog of the local landowner who had given her Harrison. She missed the lovely long rambles she and Trixxi used to take. Walking just for the sake of walking seemed so pointless, so joyless somehow, without a dog trotting along by your side, sampling all the unfamiliar smells, exploring the hedgerows, and reclaiming familiar territory. With their cheerful, rambling ways, dogs turn an ordinary walk into a happy occasion. It was true what people said, a dog does get you out and about. As she told herself that, a longing for a dog crept over her. On the other hand, they do tie you down and with the coming upheaval at the Spa, when she would no doubt have to work longer hours, she told herself sternly that this was not the right time. Still, a short walk before dinner would do her good. She slipped into a light jacket and, locking the door behind her, stepped outside just as late afternoon turned into early evening.

I can't go far, she thought, so I'll walk into town along the river and watch the sun set over the River Conwy.

She loved the river, in all its moods, although it held sad memories for her. For it was here, many years ago, that the young policeman she was in love with had drowned, saving the life of a child who had fallen in and been swept away by the strong current. She gazed at the swirling water, lost in thought, and then walked on.

As she approached the town's centuries-old three-arched bridge, Bronwyn and Robbie, out for their evening walk, crossed the town's cobbled square and headed toward her. They waited on the other side of the bridge, close to the Spa, until Penny reached them.

When she did, she bent over, gave Robbie a friendly scratch behind his ears, and then stood up and exchanged greetings with Bronwyn.

"Penny, you'll never guess who came to see me, today!"

"Ros Stephens?"

"No, that's a good guess, but no." She paused for a moment to heighten the suspense. "The bishop's wife. Yes, Pamela Blaine, herself."

"Oh, really? And am I allowed to ask what she wanted?"

"Well, I can't say too much but perhaps, since I did bring this up, after all, it would be all right for me to mention that she is in the midst of a serious marital crisis. She would like to leave the bishop; he, with one eye on keeping up appearances, is desperate to have her back."

"Then it sounds as if she holds the trump cards."

"That's what I told her. I also told her if she is to return they must negotiate a new way to be together so she gets what she wants and needs." She sighed. "But I think she will go back to him because she is afraid to be on her own. She is a woman who cannot be alone. And I expect for a time it will be different and he'll be attentive and kind, but he will gradually revert to his cold, controlling ways. But she doesn't hold all the trump cards."

"No?"

"No. He holds the guilt card over her." She lowered her voice. "Pamela had an affair and the bishop knows about it."

"Oh, I see," said Penny, not sure how much she should reveal she knew, and decided to say nothing. "That's really something, isn't it? Not what you'd expect from the wife of a bishop."

"Exactly what I thought! Anyway, must get off. It'll be dark soon and Robbie hasn't had his dinner." As the two of them trotted off, Penny walked home through the deepening dusk. Harrison would be wanting his dinner, too.

Forty-one

Well, Penny," said Mrs. Lloyd the next day, "here we are again. All that excitement at Gladstone's Library seems to be dying down, so to speak, although I understand no arrests have been made yet in the death of that Shipton chap."

"No, not yet."

"The police did interview us, Florence and me, and we told them everything we knew, but we weren't much help, I'm afraid. We were in the Gladstone Room when it happened. Florence was reading the paper and I was making sure I had the train tickets. You know how it is before a journey. You check and double check to make sure your tickets are in order. So we were waiting for the taxi to take us to the railway station, and you'd popped back to the Library, and that's when you found the body."

Penny thought about that for a moment.

"Is that what you told the police?"

"Yes."

"But Mrs. Lloyd, that was what you were doing after the murder, while I was discovering the body. What were you doing and where were you just before that? That's what the police want to know."

"Well, let me see." Her gaze wandered to the corner of the manicure room and she pursed her lips. "We talked to you in the hall about the taxi arrangements." Her brown eyes returned to Penny. "You'll remember that."

Penny nodded. "Yes, I do."

"Oh! I remember now. And after that I went back upstairs to my room. I realized I hadn't checked the en suite and I wanted to make sure I'd packed my special lavender soap that I like so much. Florence gave it to me for Christmas. It's easy to leave toiletries behind. So I went back upstairs and sure enough, I had forgotten my soap, so I tucked it in my handbag. Then I went through the door near that meeting room and started down the stairs. I was just on the landing and looking over the back garden at that peculiar statue of a half-naked woman when I heard a door slam."

"You're right! Penny exclaimed. "I heard a door slam, too. I'd forgotten about that."

"There you are then, Penny. I'm not the only one who forgets these details."

"No," said Penny, "you're not. And what happened then, Mrs. Lloyd? What happened after you heard the door slam?"

"Well, as I said, there I was on the landing and I turned around and saw someone hurrying out of the warden's office. From where I was standing I couldn't quite see properly, and I was at a little distance on the stairs looking up and the light was in my eyes so I couldn't say for sure who it was."

"But can you tell me anything about him?" asked Penny. "Let's start with that. Was it a man? Could you tell if the person was a man?"

"Yes, I think it was," Mrs. Lloyd said slowly. "And he was walking very fast. 'Purposefully,' would be the word. Yes, purposefully." And a moment later she added, with a small tremor of excitement, "and he was carrying something." She beamed at Penny. "Isn't it amazing what you can remember if you try?"

"When you say carrying something, do you mean down at his side, the way you'd carry a briefcase, say?"

"No, I mean carrying like this." Mrs Lloyd bent the elbow of her left hand and held her forearm close to her body. "Tucked in the crook of his arm, like this."

"So what would you carry like that?" Penny bent her arm toward her body.

"A stack of books?" asked Mrs. Lloyd. "Or, at least, two or three?"

Yes," said Penny, "that would make perfect sense. And anyone seen walking the halls in a library carrying a few books would attract absolutely no attention. No one would take any notice, would they?"

"Not unless it was someone who wouldn't be expected to have any books," said Mrs. Lloyd.

Penny gave her a puzzled look that cleared a moment later. "Oh, I see what you mean. Someone on the cleaning staff, for example."

"Or me!" laughed Mrs. Lloyd. "Now, Florence, no surprise there. She's down the library every week exchanging her books so if you saw her with a few books you wouldn't think twice about it. But I'm not a book reader, me. I'll stick to my magazines, thank you very much."

"But you don't know for sure that he was carrying books, do you? Could he have been carrying something else?"

Mrs. Lloyd nodded slowly. "Yes, I suppose he could have been." They fell into silence, each with her own thoughts, as Penny applied a base coat to Mrs. Lloyd's nails.

"Did we choose a colour?" Penny asked a few minutes later.

"No, we didn't. I'd like something nice and fresh for spring. Not a heavy, wintery colour."

"How about a nice, rich coral?"

"Why not?"

Penny started applying the nail varnish, while Mrs. Lloyd watched intently.

"Mrs. Lloyd?"

"Mmm?"

"Could that person coming out of the warden's office have been Hywel Stephens?"

"Well, it looked like him, I suppose, but I don't see how it could have been him. Because to come out of the warden's office he would have had to get into the warden's office and how could Hywel Stephens have got into the warden's office? Surely the door would have been locked?"

Penny gave a little exclamation of triumph.

"It's the oldest trick in the book, Mrs. Lloyd, and I'm surprised none of us thought of it before. That door that you and I heard slam . . . that was Stephens leaving the upper level of the Library through that heavy door that leads from the Library to the warden's office. It's almost as good as a secret passage. The warden liked to keep it propped open, you see, so my theory is that the killer stabbed Shipton, then slipped into the warden's office. From there, he must have gone down the hall, taken the back stairs, and disappeared. He couldn't have come down the front staircase or he would have had to pass you, and it's more likely that someone would have spotted him. But he could easily have slipped out the back way unnoticed."

"Well, I don't know. Could be, I suppose. You'll want to discuss it with that nice policeman of yours, I guess."

"Mrs. Lloyd, really, he's a very nice policeman and I know how much we all like him, but I'm sorry to have to tell that he's not my policeman. Not really. Not in the sense you mean. We're just friends."

"Really, Penny? And we all had such high hopes there. Well, if it's all over between you, I guess your sleuthing days are over, too. He'll not be passing on any more inside information. Still, probably for the best. You're going to be very busy running this place on your own now that Victoria's leaving. Where's she going? France, was it?"

Penny was aghast. "How on earth did you hear about that? As far as I know, no one's been told. We haven't even worked out the details. I don't know myself what's going to happen."

"Penny, how long have you lived here in Llanelen? Twenty-five years? You should know by now secrets don't stay secret for very long. Word gets out and when it does, it gets around very quickly."

"Italy," said Penny, grumpily. "She's going to Italy. But just for six weeks or so. Things may not work out."

"On the other hand, they very well might work out. You'd better prepare yourself just in case they do."

"Well, in the meantime, I'll tell Gareth that you saw something at the Library that could be important and I've no doubt they'll be around to reinterview you."

"That'll be fine. I like talking to him." And then she added: "Even if you don't."

Penny groaned. "Oh, Mrs. Lloyd. What are we going to do with you?"

"Well, what do you think about what Mrs. Lloyd saw?" Penny asked Davies on the telephone later that evening.

"It's something," he replied, "but it's not much to go on. We don't know who that person was or what he was carrying. At this point, I have to say the case is stalled. We've gone as far as we can."

"So what happens now?"

"We wait for the break we need to wrap things up."

Forty-two

One week later, as a full moon lit the way for clouds drifting across the midnight sky above Gladstone's Library, residents on the first floor were awakened by a loud vibrating noise. They put on dressing gowns and gathered in the hall.

"It seems to be coming from that direction," said an elderly man, pointing. Like a little flock of sheep, they shuffled toward the source of the noise. "Oh, this doesn't look good," the man said, pointing to a widening stain on the green carpet. The source of the stain seemed to be the communal shower room that was shared by two bedrooms that had not yet been retrofitted with their own en suites.

The little group stood outside the door and then a woman standing in front of it pulled the door open. The floor was flooded and a small wave of water lapped at the edge of the hall carpeting.

"I'll go downstairs and notify the person on night duty," said one resident. "I wonder if there's anything we can do to stop the flow?" asked a retired clergyman. "It looks like one for the bucket brigade until we can get the water switched off," said another.

"First the plumbers, and then the builders," said another.

An hour later, after an emergency-plumbing service had temporarily sorted out the problem, the worst of the water had been mopped up, the sodden carpet pulled back and order restored, the residents, who had all pitched in to help save their beloved library, went back to their rooms to try to get some sleep in what remained of the night.

In the morning, the builders would begin to repair the damage.

And in the morning, came the break the police were waiting for.

"We pulled the radiator out and behind it we found that," the head builder said to Davies. He pointed at a soggy clipboard and a wet book, its pages rippled and its cover warped. "Normally we wouldn't have taken any notice of it, but it's what was in the book that got our attention. We knew about the killing that happened here a few weeks back, and we thought that might be important, so we called you. It's not every day you find something like that in a book, so we knew something wasn't right."

Davies nodded. "Glad you did."

Bethan Morgan bent over and scooped up a chef's knife,

which she placed in an evidence bag, and then did the same with the book and clipboard.

"I doubt we'll find any fingerprints, but get them off to forensics, will you Bethan? Hopefully, if there's any blood from the knife on the pages of the book we'll learn something."

"Right."

"I'll have a word with the librarian. She's probably missing a book. What's the full name of it, again?"

Bethan turned the bag over so Davies could see the front of the book, with its yellow print on a blue background.

"*The Gospel According to Harry Potter. Spirituality in the stories of the world's most famous seeker.*"

"Oh, I know that book," said the librarian a few minutes later. "But I didn't realize it was missing. Well, I'm sorry to hear about the condition it's in, but I'm glad to know what happened to it so we can see about getting it replaced."

She turned to her computer and typed in an entry. "Here are its call letters." She stood up. "Follow me." They made their way carefully up to the second level and along a few rows of shelves. "Here we are," said the librarian checking the call numbers on the books and pointing to the edges of two books. "This is where the Harry Potter book used to live. Let's see if. . . ." She pushed the two books apart, reached in between the back cover of one and the front cover of its neighbour and pulled out a small piece of paper. "What's that?" asked Davies. "It's the borrower's slip. This should tell us the name of the person who signed out the Harry Potter book."

Scarcely able to believe his luck, Davies read the name: Hywel Stephens.

"May I keep this?" he asked the librarian.

"Is it a clue?" she replied with a question of her own.

"It's evidence."

Forty-three

*B*ut why on earth would he sign out a book that he was going to use to cover up a crime?" Penny asked Davies that evening.

"I wondered that, too, and the librarian said almost everyone who takes a book from the library signs for it. Even the warden. Those are the rules, and the people who are attracted to Gladstone's Library are the older, mature type who respect rules and follow them."

He took a sip of coffee. "I don't think he planned to hide the knife in the book. I think he went to the library to return the book before he left, saw Shipton, they had an argument, and he stabbed him. But we'll know more about that when we interview him."

"And when will that be?"

"Shouldn't be too long. Spain's always been a popular

destination for UK criminals on the run. Remember the good old days of the Costa del Crime? Malaga and Torremolinos were packed with British thugs and gangsters enjoying the good life under a friendly Spanish sun. But now we've got a good extradition agreement in place, and Mr. Stephens will be back with us before he knows it. In fact, I might be going there myself to fetch him back. Don't suppose you fancy a couple of days in the Marbella sunshine?"

Penny laughed and shook her head. "I can't. I don't know if I'll ever be able to get away again. We'll have to see how things go, but I'm sure Rhian will do fine as the new manager. Victoria says she's just going for six weeks or so but who knows? She might decide to trade everything here for a Tuscany farm house."

"When does she leave?"

"Saturday."

For the next minute or so, neither spoke. Then, Penny asked about the knife that had been used to kill Shipton.

"But why was he walking around with a chef's knife? Where did he get it? From the kitchen?"

"No. But coincidentally, the kitchen was missing a knife at that time so we thought we were looking for a kitchen knife. But it turned out the weekend chef had put the knife in the wrong drawer and it turned up. But they forgot to let us know. We checked all the details of the kitchen operations and it would be difficult for someone to just wander into that kitchen and take a knife. Despite what happened to Minty Russell—her allergy poisoning was an insider job, if you will—it's a safe, professional, well-run kitchen."

"So where did the knife come from?"

"Stephens bought it at the Tesco down the road that

morning. We'll find out for sure, but it may be that one of his wives asked him to pick one up." He shrugged. "As I said, we'll know more after we've interviewed him, including why he killed Shipton." He stood up. "But I suspect the motive will come down to money."

"Money?"

"He's an accountant. His whole world is money."

Minty's sister Constance had lost weight and her face was now gaunt and hollow. She spent most days in the bed that had been set up for her in the sitting room and her husband, Elwy, had arranged for a neighbour to look in on her in the afternoons when he was at work. He had explained to the pub manager that he could no longer work evenings or nights because of his wife's illness.

She stirred as the front door opened and came fully awake at the sound of a banging, thumping noise. "Hello, love, only me," her husband called as he entered the room. He bent over and kissed her forehead.

"What was all that banging about?" his wife asked.

"Oh, that," her husband said. "The funeral director called to apologize. Apparently there was some mix up with the police and they've only now just got round to releasing Minty's possessions. I had to go and pick them up." He pointed to the sad little black case standing in the hall. "Shall I bring it in? Do you feel up to going through it?"

"Never mind that now, Elwy. I want to talk to you. It's important."

"What is it, love?" he said pulling a chair closer to his bed side. "Are you feeling poorly?'

"You could say that, you bloody great lummox. Yes, I'm feeling poorly. In fact, Elwy, I'm preparing to die."

"Oh, don't talk so. You'll outlive us all, see if you don't."

"Elwy, please, I need you to listen to me. When you deny what I'm saying like that, it's to make you feel better because you don't want to acknowledge the truth. But you need to hear me. You need to listen."

He did not reply.

"I want you to ask the rector from St. Deiniol's next door to the Library to come and see me. I want to talk to him. Will you do that?" He nodded. "And I've got to make a will. I always thought I'd go first, not Minty. So you need to ask the lawyer to come and see me, too. There are things that need to be taken care of. It's time for me to put my affairs in order." She held up a thin hand to silence Elwy's protest.

"Now, I know mother and Minty had no use for you, and there have been times when I wasn't so sure myself, but I've got no one else, except you, Elwy. And you've been so good to me these past few weeks, I'm starting to wonder if they were wrong about you. So I'm going to leave everything, well, what there is, to you."

She stopped and closed her eyes. "Do you want a drink of water, love?" he asked.

She nodded and sat up slightly. He poured some water into a glass and inserted a bendy straw and held it to her lips. "Take your time, love. No hurry."

"Well, I guess you might as well open Minty's suitcase now so we can see what's in it," she said.

He turned the case on its side and using both hands

yanked the two zipper pulls away from each other, then flipped the lid open. He picked through a few items of clothing, Minty's eyeglasses, some toiletry items, and then pulled out a blue velvet box with a silver clasp. He opened it with a smile and tipped it so Constance could see the contents. "Here you go, dear. Your mother's pearls. Would you like me to help you put them on?"

"They were granny's pearls, actually," said Constance, leaning forward so he could slip them behind her neck and fasten the clasp. When he finished, she sat back, and lovingly held the triple strand of pale cream pearls, rolling them gently between her fingers and thumb. "From Granny, to mother, to Minty, to me. It's too bad I'll never have the chance to wear them properly. Somewhere nice." She gave him a weak smile, sighed, and closed her eyes. "I'd love to wear them to a tea dance, if they still held such things. Such a lovely idea, don't you think? A tea dance." Her husband sat in silence, waiting and watching.

A few moments later her eyelids fluttered open and she seemed to gather strength.

"So, Elwy, as I said, I'm going to leave everything to you. Except for one thing. The pearls."

"Well, I don't have much use for them, do I?"

"No, and I don't want some fancy woman you take up with after I'm gone getting her hands on them." He seemed about to say something and then thought better of it. "Just listen to me, Elwy. I wish I had a daughter or even a niece to leave the pearls to, but I don't. I've given this a lot of thought and this is what I'd like to do with them. I want to leave them to the church. That way, any bride being married there could borrow them to wear on her wedding day.

They would be known as St. Deiniol's pearls. They would be the 'something borrowed.' What do you think of that idea?"

"I think it's a wonderful idea, love. They'll look as beautiful on the St. Deiniol's brides as they do on you."

Elwy gave the blue box a little shake. The pearls had sat on a false bottom. He lifted it up and pulled out a piece of paper. He unfolded it and showed it to his wife. "What do you make of that?" he asked.

"It's just a bunch of numbers," she shrugged "with that one number highlighted at the bottom, see? I have no idea what it means. Just something Minty was working on when she died, I guess. Means nothing to us, and it can't have been that important or the police would have found it when they went through her things. Put it in the recycling, and then put the kettle on. But first, tell me what you did at work today. Did anyone interesting come into the pub?"

"A Canadian woman. Red hair. Said she'd been doing some sketching and drawing at the Library."

"Oh. A tourist, I guess. Bit early for them, but it's May, so they do start to arrive about now, tourists."

"Maybe she was a tourist, but I don't think so. She seemed to know her way around. Said she'd stopped at the Library several times now and how much she loved it."

"Oh. I guess it would be too much of a coincidence if she'd been at the Library in April when Minty was there. If she'd been there when all that awful business happened."

"Yes, that would be too much of a coincidence. Things like that might happen in books, but they don't happen in real life, do they, pet?"

"No, I guess not."

"Well, love, you just sit back and relax and I'll put the kettle on."

After a cold, wet April, the flowers of May were especially welcome. Penny packed a picnic lunch for two, her sketching supplies, and with Davies beside her, they set off for Parc Mawr. Loping along at their side was Trixxi, the black lab she adored who had been left in her care for a few days while her owner was away.

They'd had a couple of honest, intense talks over the past few days and reached a quiet understanding. Penny had opened up and explained that she liked her life the way it was and felt she had lived on her own for too long to create a new, intimate life with someone else.

Davies had said he respected her all the more for her candour.

But if she had told him what the relationship would not be, they had yet to define what it would be. And that, they'd both agreed, might take some time.

Penny smiled to herself. Even though their future was still uncertain, she felt more at ease with him than she had for a while.

At the Woodland Trust area, the forest floor was carpeted as far as the eye could see with a shimmering drift of bluebells. Grateful for the cloudy day that allowed the flowers to be seen at their purest blue, Penny took out her notepad and with rapid, sure strokes began to capture the bluebells' bright beauty.

She took a few photographs to use later, to remind her of the depth of the colour, when she turned her sketches into watercolour paintings. And then, because Trixxi was anxious for the walk to continue, the three moved on. The days were warm now, with summer just around the corner.

They talked about Victoria, who was happy in Italy. Penny was starting to accept that she might not be back, and to think about what that would mean for her. The Spa was doing well under Rhian's management, and its reputation was growing.

They stopped for lunch by a small stream that gave a spectacular view over the valley to the ancient hills beyond. Davies had returned yesterday from Spain, where he'd interviewed Hywel Stephens, who had confessed to the murder of Nigel Shipton but showed very little remorse, just as he'd showed very little remorse for the hurt he'd caused his family. "He's not sorry for what he did," Davies said. "He's sorry he got caught."

"Why did he do it?" Penny asked. "Was it about the money?"

"Yes and no," Davies replied. "He did need the money from his partnership with Shipton to maintain his two families, but the murder wasn't just about money. It was about protecting his secret."

"His secret? You mean the family in Spain?" asked Penny.

"No. He was having an affair with another woman, closer to home. Shipton found out and threatened to tell the woman's husband."

"Really."

"Hmm."

He picked up a piece of sliced apple and bit the end off it.

"By the way, did you know Pamela Blaine's mobile phone number was almost identical to your landline?"

"Really?"

"Yeah, the one she was using until a few weeks ago. Just one digit difference. Her phone number ended in a six. Yours ends in a nine. I recognized the similarity right away when we were sorting through her calls."

Penny started to laugh.

"What is it?"

"I was just thinking what a huge difference that one number made. And it was an accountant, of all people, who got his numbers mixed up and dialed nine for murder."

He threw her a quizzical look.

"Oh, didn't I tell you? I came home from work one day and there was a voice-mail message . . . a wrong number, obviously . . . about a conference at a library. . . ."